The Gentleman Thief

A Christian Regency Adventure
novella

Lady Wynwood's Spies series
Prequel

Camille Elliot

Camy Tang

P.O. Box 23143

San Jose, CA 95153-3143

www.camilleelliot.com

Publisher's Note: This is a work of fiction. Names, characters, places, and incidents are a product of the author's imagination. Locales and public names are sometimes used for atmospheric purposes. Any resemblance to actual people, living or dead, or to businesses, companies, events, institutions, or locales is completely coincidental.

The Gentleman Thief/ Camille Elliot. — 1st ed.

eBook ISBN 978-1-942225-20-1

Print ISBN 978-1-942225-19-5

This is a prequel novella to my Christian Regency Romantic Adventure series, Lady Wynwood's Spies. It takes place after the events of *The Spinster's Christmas* but before *Lady Wynwood's Spies, volume 1: Archer.*

Lady Wynwood's Spies series

Recommended reading order

The Spinster's Christmas (prequel)
The Gentleman Thief (prequel novella)
Lady Wynwood's Spies, volume 1: Archer
Lady Wynwood's Spies, volume 2: Berserker
Lady Wynwood's Spies, volume 3: Aggressor
Lady Wynwood's Spies, volume 4: Betrayer
Lady Wynwood's Spies, volume 5: Prisoner
Lady Wynwood's Spies, volume 6: Martyr
Lady Wynwood's Spies, volume 7: Spinster (coming soon)

Standalone novels

Prelude for a Lord
The Gentleman's Quest

Devotional

Who I Want to Be

Chapter One

The magical night was awash with diamonds.

Perhaps because the party was being held by Mr. Holmendale, an avid collector of rare diamonds, all the women had donned their most glittering diamonds for the party. Very few dared to wear colored stones, considered inferior by the wealthy Mr. Holmendale, and so even Rheda's mother had unearthed her grandmother's truly ugly diamond parure and flaunted the gaudy pieces with a pride she surely did not feel.

Rheda was forced to wear nothing, since their host would sniff at her if she wore her chaste pearls, but she didn't mind. The pearl necklace was a tiny bit snug around her throat and she hated the feeling of being choked. It made her feel breathless. However, her mother often told her that she felt breathless because she couldn't stop talking.

But Rheda couldn't help herself. It was her first Season in London, and everything was new and exciting. What was especially exciting was that Rheda had Fallen in Love.

It had been at her first ball, when she'd been a bundle of nerves. Her eye had fallen on a slender boy, perhaps eighteen or nineteen, his shoulders hunched as he slouched in a corner, likely trying to remain unnoticed by the hostess so he wouldn't have to dance. His very defiance of convention made her heart swell. Then he'd turned and happened to see her, and she felt it must be fate.

His golden-brown eyes found hers, and she fell deeply in love.

It was even more endearing that he'd immediately blushed to the tips of his ears. It didn't matter that he'd glared and frowned at her, then turned brusquely away.

Rheda's heart was caught and would be His Forever.

And now she was actually attending a party at his house! Well, it belonged to his father, Mr. Holmendale, but that only meant that his son, Mr. Kent Holmendale, was guaranteed to be attending.

Rheda's one wish for this evening was that Mr. Kent Holmendale would ask her to dance.

She knew she had to work on him, like their chef worked on the dough that became Rheda's favorite Uxbridge cakes. She would have to tease and cajole him, but she was determined to be victorious tonight and secure that dance. She had told her best friend Miss Reed—or had it been her other best friend Miss Alexander? Or had it been her *other* best friend Miss Powell? Well, she had told one of them that she would *force*—er, convince Mr. Kent Holmendale to ask her to dance this very evening. All her hopes would finally be realized!

The Season was still young, that was true—in fact, it had not officially begun, and these engagements were more like delicacies to whet the appetite before a sumptuous banquet. So she had plenty of time to capture his heart ... but sooner was always better than later!

She and her family stood in line on the stairs for what seemed like forever and a day. At last they reached the head of the receiving line and were greeted by Mr. and Mrs. Holmendale. The hostess of the evening was positively dripping in diamonds, from her tiara to the buckles on her shoes. Rheda's eyes felt as if she might go blind by the splendor of it all. But she managed a bright smile and what she hoped was a deep enough curtsey before her gaze wandered behind them to the ballroom beyond. Her mother elbowed her sharply and frowned at her, so she must have been too obvious that her attention was focused elsewhere.

Rheda had only met Mrs. Holmendale once at a party, and very briefly, but now she was surprised when that lady gave her a V-shaped smile. Her narrow eyes narrowed even further until they were nearly slits in her face, giving her a very sly look. "Well, well, miss, I can wager what drew you here this evening," she teased Rheda.

"I do beg your pardon, Mrs. Holmendale," Rheda's mother said in mortified tones.

"Ah, to be young again." Mrs. Holmendale's smile widened further as she looked at Rheda again. "Well, do go and *run him to ground.*"

Rheda had no more thought than to bob another quick curtsey and dart into the ballroom. The hostess had given her permission, after all! How delightful! True, Mrs. Holmendale's expression had been a bit crafty, but an elegant woman like that wouldn't have a crafty bone in her body. Rheda was simply imagining it.

The ballroom was already unbearably crowded, despite the fact that town was only partially filled with people come to enjoy the Season. Rheda saw that there were multitudes of spindly trees placed around the room, with settees planted between the large pots and draped with moss-green fabric as if to give the impression the guest had walked into a garden, but it also served to shrink the area available for people to stand and mingle.

Rheda had to squeeze quite close between clusters of people to move through. She received a few irritated looks, but she was in a hurry! She had no time for polite "excuse me"s when her object was True Love!

She found her Darling Kent—she had not the courage to say his name in public, but in her mind he was her Darling Kent—

slinking behind several of the trees, with two other young men by his side. But compared to Kent's glorious face and figure, the other two were mere striplings and unworthy of her notice. Kent was the epitome of a brooding, romantic male figure. Hearts around the room would sigh with delight if he'd only step out from behind that tree.

"Mr. Holmendale!" When she broke into their conversational circle and said his name, it came out rather breathy. She hoped she didn't sound insipid. "How lovely to see you again."

Kent's eyes had flown to hers when she interrupted them, and they widened upon seeing her. Ah! He must be pleased to see her, too!

"It is such a privilege to be in your company tonight. You are looking quite dashing. I do hope you have been enjoying yourself so far. I have only just arrived with my mama, but she will likely take herself off to the card room immediately. She always does so. She says she is quite gifted at whist, although I have not seen it when I am forced to play across from her. Do you play whist, Mr. Holmendale?"

She had that breathless feeling again, and this time she wasn't wearing her pearls! How strange. Perhaps Mama was right and she was speaking too fast. Or had she said that Rheda spoke too much, not too fast? Either way, she had to pause to catch her breath.

"Kent, do introduce this little kitten," one of the young men said. He had a smile on his face, but it seemed to be aimed more at Kent than at her. If he'd been attempting to flirt with her, she would have put him on the roundabout directly.

Her Darling Kent frowned at his friend, and he said reluctantly, "Jonas, Simon, this is Miss Isherwood. Miss Isherwood, this is Mr. Jonas Sneed and Mr. Simon Eggerton."

Was he perhaps jealous he had to share her with them? How wonderful! But she would not tease him and flirt with his friends, because her heart was Forever His. "It is a pleasure to meet you both," she said with a polite curtsey, but her attention was immediately returned to her Darling Kent. "I have heard that your mother has allowed dancing for tonight. I do hope you intend to dance, Mr. Holmendale. I have seen you dance a few times and you are wonderfully graceful and light on your feet."

For some reason, her words made Mr. Sneed and Mr. Eggerton snort with laughter. Mr. Sneed even jabbed an elbow in Mr. Holmendale's side, which Rheda thought was very rude. Mr. Holmendale, forbearing and kind as he was, didn't even reprimand them for their behavior, but instead turned his face away from them. Surely he thought their behavior beneath his notice, although strangely, his face had turned a rather rosy pink color.

"Alas, I have no one to dance with me." She lowered her eyes in the way that her best friend Miss Croft—or was it her other best friend Miss Davis?—had said was guaranteed to be irresistible to men. "It is my first Season, and so I am acquainted with very few people."

Her Darling Kent's eyes suddenly alighted with ... well, she thought at first it might be mischief, but her Darling Kent wouldn't wish to cause her mischief, so she thought she must be mistaken. He must be eager to raise her from the Depths of her Social Isolation, because he said, "I say, Miss Isherwood, I'm certain Jonas and Simon would be happy to dance with you. They're both so much more *light on their feet* than myself." He gave them what other women might interpret as a smirk, but her Darling Kent was only trying to share his delight in his excellent idea with his friends.

He was so pleased with his plan that she hadn't the heart to tell him that it was himself she wished to dance with! He was being so very kind to her and to his friends, whom she was certain must be social pariahs from the way they were looking so choked right now. Any young woman would think they were very peculiar and would avoid them like the plague.

"Where is your dance card, Miss Isherwood?" Mr. Holmendale asked. "Jonas and Simon should be happy to sign it right now."

She produced the little card, given to her at the door and tied around her wrist, with a fair bit of reluctance. She had no wish to dance with such odd boys! She wanted to dance with her Darling Kent! She was struck with a terrible thought. Would dancing with these awkward young men cause her reputation to plummet? Would other women see her as one of those desperate girls who could only secure dances with equally desperate men? While she had no plans to become the reigning belle of the Season, she had a reputation to maintain. Dancing with these queer boys (who looked half-witted to boot!) might make the other girls laugh at her behind their fans!

But she didn't truly care about anyone else's opinion besides her Darling Kent, did she? And she would be doing his friends a Great Favor by dancing with them. She might even condescend to introduce them to some of her less fortunate friends who were in need of dance partners.

She hadn't quite given her dance card to her Darling Kent when there was the sound of a loud bell, and she quickly snatched the card back as they all turned toward the front of the room, where Kent's father was standing. Saved by the official start of the party! Rheda nearly gusted a sigh of relief, but reminded herself just in time that it was an uncouth action for which her mother would have scolded her.

"Friends," Mr. Holmendale called to the hushed room, "I thank you for joining me this evening for this auspicious occasion. I had never thought to one day be throwing this grand fete for this wonderful purpose, the purchase of the crowning jewel of my collection, a piece for which I have long coveted and searched the world over. Later this evening, you shall all be given an opportunity to see my latest acquisition, the Isadora

Diamond!"

At his last words, servants around the hall tugged at silken cords that Rheda hadn't noticed were draped down from white silk bundles on the ceiling. At the servants' motions, the silk cords loosed the white silk and long strings of diamonds cascaded down from where they were suspended above the guests. The diamond strings glittered in the candlelight and turned the ballroom into a magical fairyland of sparkling light.

"Oh! Oh!" Rheda was nearly speechless with delight. "How magnificent! How dramatic! Oh, I see, it is to celebrate your father's newest diamond, is it not? Mr. Holmendale, how clever! Did you think of such a thing? How lovely!"

Even his friends seemed impressed by the display, although after a moment, they erased their expressions of surprise with masks of boredom. Rheda thought they were being very silly. As if boredom made them more fashionable! Why not show how delighted they were? She would like them much better if they were not trying so desperately to be unimpressed.

Her Darling Kent's expression remained surly, since he had surely known about the surprise. At least he did not pretend to be bored. Her Darling Kent always seemed to show exactly what he was thinking.

"I say," Mr. Sneed said, "Since the diamond hanging-things are interfering with the dancing area, does that mean there won't be any dancing?"

"How tragic!" Rheda exclaimed. "Say that isn't so, Mr. Holmendale?"

Her Darling Kent gave a long-suffering sigh. "Of course there's still dancing, Jonas. Get your head on straight. The couples are supposed to pass through the strings of diamonds."

"Those aren't real diamonds, are they?" Mr. Eggerton asked.

"Of course not," Kent said. "They're paste. I had to help Mother string them up this afternoon."

"Such a help for his mama," Mr. Eggerton teased with his

mouth puckered.

"Indeed, a man who helps his mother is most worthy of respect!" Rheda answered hotly.

For some reason, that made his friends laugh again, and Kent's face became more pink, revealing whitish splotches across his cheeks. Rheda found it adorable.

"Hey, let's see that diamond," Mr. Sneed said.

"You can't wait until later?" Kent asked in an annoyed tone.

"Don't want to," Mr. Sneed said with a cheeky grin.

"Hey, you can open the safe where it's kept, can't you?" Mr. Eggerton asked.

"Yes, you have access, surely?" Mr. Sneed's eyes had narrowed and his smile looked challenging rather than friendly.

"Of course I do," Kent snapped, although his eyes shifted sideways and he looked uncomfortable.

"You mustn't do anything that would cause your mother or father to become upset with you," Rheda said.

"Oh, of course," Mr. Sneed said quickly, although the innocence on his face had a sharp, snide tinge. "You must only ever be a good, obedient boy."

Her Darling Kent's face flushed dark red, making the whitish splotches turn light pink. "I'm not afraid of my father."

"I didn't say you were." Mr. Sneed's innocent-yet-somehow-snide look didn't change.

"If you want to look at the diamond, let's look at the diamond." He turned to leave the ballroom.

"We needn't do it now," Mr. Eggerton said, with a sidelong glare at Mr. Sneed.

"If you want to see it, come now," Kent growled. "Otherwise, wait your turn with everyone else." The last was thrown over his shoulder almost like a threat at Mr. Sneed, whose smile widened.

"By all means, let's view the legendary diamond." Mr. Sneed offered his arm to Rheda, whose opinion of him rose a notch.

"Miss Isherwood?"

"Thank you," she said primly, although privately she thought they ought not to be doing this. Won't her Darling Kent become the object of his father's wrath for touching such a magnificent treasure without permission? But he seemed confident he had the right to do so. Perhaps her fears were all for naught.

"Are you certain you wish to see the Isadora Diamond, Miss Isherwood?" asked Mr. Eggerton.

"Whyever not?" She was only half-listening to Mr. Eggerton, for they were passing through the hallway that ran outside the length of the ballroom, and the portraits on the wall were quite ridiculous. Old men and women in outmoded costumes, either so plain and austere that they were hopelessly boring, or else far too little lace and ribbons on the women and far too many on the men.

"Why, haven't you heard?" Mr. Sneed's smile seemed sly again. "The Isadora Diamond is rumored to be cursed."

"Cursed?" Rheda had to admit that she felt a twinge of … well, certainly not *fear*, but slight discomfort in her breast at the word. "How did it become cursed? Someone cursed it for some reason? A diamond simply cannot come out of the ground already cursed. No one has done anything to it, and it hasn't done anything to anyone."

Her Darling Kent burst out laughing, and the sound was like music to her ears. Mr. Sneed looked disgruntled, and she realized he had been hoping to scare her. Well, Rheda Isherwood was not easily frightened! Indeed, she was the only one of her cousins who could stand to kill the spiders in the rooms at their grandparents' home.

Mr. Eggerton was also smiling at her. "Supposedly a witch used the Isadora Diamond and two other gemstones in a spell, causing the death of her entire village."

Rheda shuddered a bit. Spiders were one thing, but witches

made her shiver.

No, she was Rheda Isherwood! She was not some lily-livered debutante. She had the bravery gifted to her by the power of True Love! "That is nonsense," she said.

"I assure you, it is true," Mr. Sneed said, his serpentine smile back in place.

"Of course it isn't," she said. "Witches are nasty, poor creatures with bad hair. A witch wouldn't have gotten her hands on a priceless diamond, much less three of them. If she really wanted revenge, she could have sold the diamonds and bought out the village and made them into her serfs. I assure you, any woman would rather have servants at her beck and call than an entire dead village."

She was rewarded when her Darling Kent laughed again. He really became sinfully handsome when he laughed. Why, his brown eyes turned almost gold. She determined to do everything in her power to make him laugh more.

They had traversed the hallway and descended a narrow set of servants' stairs. They now followed the twisted paths of darker, narrower halls before finding their way back to the main hallway on the floor below the ballroom. It was eerily quiet without the murmur of voices, and since the dancing had not yet started, there was no music from the musicians filtering down through the floor.

Her Darling Kent led them to a heavy wooden door on the left, but when he tried to open it, it wouldn't budge.

"Got the key?" Mr. Sneed somehow made his question sound like an insult.

"He didn't lock it earlier." Kent rattled the door. "Sometimes it gets stuck and you have to lift up …" He jerked upward on the knob and the door gave a little jump, then swung open. He sneered at Mr. Sneed. "See?"

Mr. Sneed said nothing as he escorted Rheda inside. Her Darling Kent followed, then walked past them to the far corner of the study.

The study had much fewer books than Rheda would have expected, only one large bookshelf behind the massive oak desk and a smaller circular shelf in the corner next to a globe. The wallpaper was striped green and very plain, but also very rich-looking. The rest of the walls were covered in hunting scenes, and several chairs and a sofa sat in front of a huge fireplace across from the desk.

Kent had gone to the far corner, but now he stood staring dumbly at the wall. Rheda hurried forward. Perhaps he was frightened by a spider! She could catch it and kill it directly, and he would be ever so grateful and take her in his arms …

She never got farther than that in her daydream because she was shocked by the hole in the wall, near the base. No, not a hole—a wooden panel had curiously been set in the green-striped wall, but now it swung outward, revealing a small square space. A large safe box had been set in the space, except that the door for that, too, was swung open.

"It's gone." Kent's voice was stunned and hollow. "The Isadora Diamond."

"It's been stolen?" Mr. Eggerton's voice rose in alarm.

Rheda let out a piercing scream. "There are burglars in the house!"

It really was not Rheda's fault that her scream had been so loud. The boys all flinched and grabbed their ears, then started yelling at Rheda about losing their hearing. She didn't pay attention to them because she was running out of the room, shrieking about burglars.

Luckily, a servant heard her and ran off to tell the master, while some maids came and soothed her frayed sensibilities.

She only realized later with disappointment that she should have remained with her Darling Kent, clinging to his arm and weeping. Her best friend Miss Mosely—or was it her other best friend Miss Turner?—had told her that she looked quite beautiful when she cried.

Alas, she was only able to observe him from a distance when his father was summoned and he saw the opened safe for himself. He was quite cruel to Her Darling Kent and yelled at him with embarrassing force. Rheda was about to rush to Kent's side when his mother arrived and calmly took control of the situation.

Of course, Rheda understood that the ball was completely ruined by the theft of the star of the evening, but really, there could have still been *some* dancing. After all, Mr. Holmendale had already paid for the magnificent decorations and the musicians.

But instead, she and her party were forced to stand and wait in the overcrowded foyer with all the other guests after Mrs. Holmendale bid them a hasty goodbye. Mr. Holmendale was inconsolable, pale and shaking as he sat in a chair in the now-empty ballroom.

Soon Rheda and her party were trundled off into their carriage.

"Good gracious, Mr. Allinton," her mother said to their guest. "How disappointing that your first entertainment in London this Season should be so shocking." Her mother, however, was practically beaming. She'd have a juicy story to tell her friends who hadn't been able to receive an invitation to Mr. Holmendale's celebratory ball, and they would positively fawn over her for details.

"I shall have a truly captivating tale for my next letter to Mr. Jacob Isherwood," Mr. Allinton said. He had arrived in town just last week, and a chance meeting with Rheda and her mother at a bookshop had led to Mrs. Isherwood begging him to escort them to the Holmendale ball, assuring him that Mrs. Holmendale would not mind his presence since Rheda's father was unable to accompany them. Mr. Allinton was apparently a very good friend of Rheda's Uncle Jacob, although she couldn't remember ever meeting him before a few days ago.

Rheda's mother and Mr. Allinton gossiped quite shamelessly on their way to his townhouse. His address was a step up from the rented townhouse Mrs. Isherwood had been able to procure for Rheda's debut Season, but much smaller. He was apparently from a very wealthy family, which bought him access to the most exclusive events of the Season, but his family also engaged in Trade. Her mother had said the word in a scandalized whisper, so Rheda assumed it was a Bad Thing.

Mr. Allinton bid the Isherwoods goodbye and thanked them graciously for both the ride and the entree into Mr. Holmendale's aborted party. Mrs. Isherwood was already scheming about whom she would call upon tomorrow to tell them about the evening.

Rheda sighed as they pulled away from his home. Her evening had been Perfectly Ruined!

As Stewart Allinton turned toward his townhouse, he reached into his jacket pocket. Yes, it was still there.

He fingered the large diamond he'd slipped inside.

Chapter Two

Mr. Solomon Drydale lightly climbed the shallow steps to the entrance to his club, the Ivory Ramparts, which was situated on a respectable street off of Pall Mall. It was not as exclusive, nor did it encourage the deep play of clubs such as White's, Brook's, and Boodle's, but he had been a member for two decades, and it was a comfortable place.

Within, the "ivory ramparts" had been erected in the form of numerous games of chess. Some members played in the more casual outer room, while the more serious games were staged in the inner room barricaded by a thick door to block all sound.

Sol entered the large outer room that fronted the street, bright with the light from the numerous windows, enhanced by the occasional strategically-placed brace of candles. As he passed through the sea of chairs and tables, he was hailed by a group of acquaintances he'd known when they'd fought in the army together close to twenty years ago. He greeted them, but did not stop to chat. Sir Derrick would be waiting, and one did not make him wait.

The far door opened to a hallway with some private rooms, each heavy wooden door closed and the darkness lit by only six braces of candles that ran down the walls. Sol made for the second to the last room on the left.

The room had been reserved, but it was empty. Like the other private rooms, it did not contain a window, but it was the smallest among them, with barely space for a tiny table and two chairs, both of them dark wood but not as comfortable as the leather chairs in the other rooms of the club. Sol barely glanced at them and instead made his way to the far wall.

This wall of the club was shared by the building next door, which was a small haberdasher's shop. Despite the competition of other shops frequented by various noble personages, this haberdasher's always seemed to squeak by year after year. Sol had visited the shop only last week and walked out with his new hat.

The private room was painted a dark beige only along the top foot or so. The majority of the walls had been paneled with intricately hand-carved wood, giving it a sumptuous feel but making it a darker space. So it was difficult to notice the small section of carved wood that could slide to the side, revealing a keyhole. Sol used his pewter key, and the door, covered with panels so that it was completely hidden, swung into the space beyond.

He was greeted by the usual friendly smile of a woman known only as "Miss Nell," who sat at a desk directly to the side of the doorway, and by her decidedly not-friendly pistol trained at him. The room beyond was brighter than the one he'd exited, so his eyes were dazzled and he couldn't see her very well in the first few moments, but he spoke into the bright candlelight, "Good morning, Miss Nell," as he carefully shut the door behind him.

There was the sound of heavy metal hitting a wooden desk with a soft *thud*. "Good morning, Mr. Drydale. He's waiting for you." Miss Nell then continued with some paperwork before her. As a doorkeeper, she was deceptively small and plain-looking, with brown hair and brown eyes and a neat brown dress, but her proficiency with that pistol within the department was the stuff of legend. Because of the nature of her job, she was also the appointments secretary for Sol's superiors.

The long, windowless room where Miss Nell sat looked like any gentleman's club room, with a fireplace and chairs situated in intimate gatherings. Once in a while, Sol saw an agent or two talking quietly in a corner or in front of the fireplace, but he rarely tarried here. He crossed the space to one of the three doors in the opposite wall.

It led only to a narrow stairwell, and he climbed to the first floor where it opened into a very dark hallway with doors set at intervals. He entered the third on his left.

Sir Derrick Bayberry's office was filled with papers—on the desk, on the chairs, in the bookcases that lined three walls. And yet they were all neatly stacked, some in leather folios, some in stiff pasteboard boxes. The sheer amount of printed word was staggering, but Bayberry was known to reach into a stack—sometimes barely looking—and remove the information he needed.

Sol bowed at the door, but Sir Derrick waved him in impatiently even as he continued scrawling on a piece of notepaper in front of him. After the door was closed, he pointed imperiously at the chair opposite the desk, all without looking up.

However, once Sol sat down, Sir Derrick's attention was focused completely upon him. The large, slightly protuberant dark brown eyes regarded him intently, the whites strangely bright in contrast to the tanned color of his skin, a rarity among the pasty-white gentlemen of London. Despite the fact he was only a few years older than Sol, his head was almost completely bald, and with his sharp nose made him look distinctly hawk-like.

"Well?" Sir Derrick barked.

"We've been through all the men on the list and eliminated five of them. I also spoke extensively with Sir Horace Bigby at Christmastide and searched his room, and I believe we may eliminate him, as well. But we're at a loss as to how to eliminate or confirm the rest."

"All their homes have been searched?"

"Yes, sir." Twice, in fact.

Sir Derrick sighed heavily. "It's been eight months. We must find that mole soon."

"I only have the one agent to help me keep an eye on all the men on the shortlist you gave to me. And ..." Sol grimaced. "It is possible that there are other men within the Foreign Office who could have arranged for that message to be sent to Napoleon's aide."

"I will look into any other men not on the list who should be added to it." Sir Derrick gave him a baleful glance. "You need to expand your team."

"This issue is too sensitive. I've had to carefully assess possible agents, but too many have connections to the Foreign Office."

His superior rubbed his tired eyes with his hands. He hated wearing his reading glasses, but like Sol, age was catching up to him. "I know you must be careful. The wrong man could collapse your investigation and destroy this entire department with it. But this matter cannot be drawn out much longer."

"I am aware of that, sir." His frustration leaked out in his tone, and he regretted his retort.

Sir Derrick, however, did not take offense. "I have a report that might interest you, and you will be able to work with two agents to get a measure of their character. I can vouch for them both, although they are not quite the type you are accustomed to working with."

"I am not averse to unconventional agents."

Sir Derrick barked a laugh. "Yes, that is true. Here." He slid a leather folio across the desk to Sol, who opened it.

In the past several weeks during the sparse social whirl before the Season fully began, there had been three thefts that occurred during parties. Two thefts had been discovered after the guests had left, but only a few nights ago in the middle of Mr. Holmendale's ball, the theft had been made public when his son had come upon the empty safe.

"A safe," Sol murmured. In all three thefts, safe boxes had been broken into and a rare, exquisite gemstone had been stolen.

"Yes," Sir Derrick said, "I know very few men who can break into safe boxes with such skill and speed."

"Allinton." A young agent whom Sol himself had trained. "But he retired years ago. He has a family now, and a house in the country. He hasn't been to town since his marriage."

"That's what I thought, but then I did some poking around personally."

Which often meant that Sir Derrick used some of his connections in the nobility. Many of the agents currently in the department did not necessarily have close connections to the peerage, so when it came to investigating titled gentlemen, the duty often fell to either Sol or Sir Derrick.

Sir Derrick continued, "I admit I steered the conversations, but I discovered from different people that Allinton was seen at all three of the parties."

"Since ..." Sol glanced at the pages. "... three weeks ago?"

"Yes, although I heard from Mrs. Isherwood that he claimed to have been back in town only for a week. He got himself invited to the Holmendale ball through his connection to the Isherwoods. In fact, when I went to talk to people currently in town who have some family connection to Allinton, I discovered that he used his other family and friends to gain admittance to the other two events."

"Has anyone else made the connection between Allinton and the thefts?"

"I doubt it. He was not invited to any of the events, and so his name was not on the guest list. No one else knows about his skill with safe boxes, and while one person might have seen him at one event, they did not see him at another. I suppose if someone were well-connected in society and put together all the disparate stories ... *and* if they had a reason to suspect the great-grandson of an earl, they might figure it out, but ..."

"It may not be him." Sol knew he was grasping at straws. "It could have been someone from a number of criminal gangs."

"Incidentally ..." Sir Derrick drawled the word out. "A week before the first theft, a man was arrested at the home of the first victim, attempting to break into his safe."

"Who?"

"You might know him as ..." Sir Derrick cleared his throat. "Bob the Minotaur."

Sol winced. Bob's grandiose name nonetheless demanded respect from among the criminals in London because he was known to be the very best at breaking into safe boxes. His record was up to forty-five, if rumor were to be believed. Before he retired, Allinton's total had been thirty-seven.

"So Bob was finally caught?"

"He crept into the house at night to try to open the safe and steal the rare sapphire inside, but he was caught by servants when they heard noises in the house." Sir Derrick's expression grew a little pained. "Bob's apparently going a bit deaf, according to the agent who questioned him."

That might be why Bob was known to avoid face-to-face meetings with clients, and often only communicated with letters. "Bob said nothing about who hired him?"

"The old goat is as stubborn as one, probably because he thinks he'll be released, since he didn't actually steal anything. The only reason we know he wanted the sapphire was because it was the only thing of value in the safe he was trying to open."

Sol looked at the report. "And then a week later, the sapphire was successfully stolen. And then two more gemstones."

Sir Derrick slid another paper over the desk toward him. "I

discovered that he has accepted an invitation to Lady Meynhill's birthday celebration next week, at Helsey Park."

"But Lord Meynhill doesn't own any rare gemstones."

"Allinton may not be after a gemstone."

"I don't understand why he'd steal anything," Sol said. "I trained the man. I worked with him. There must be a mistake."

"There might be," Sir Derrick conceded. "Which is why I want you to bring him in. Can you get an invitation to Meynhill's party? I heard it's a grand house party."

Sol knew all about the event because his friend, Lady Wynwood, was even now preparing to leave town to attend. "Yes, I believe so." He'd need to come up with a good excuse to go, since Laura knew he wasn't overly fond of house parties.

"I know this is a departure from your search for the mole," Sir Derrick said, "but Allinton's behavior is strange. I wouldn't want just anyone to try to capture him."

"Of course, sir."

As Sol left the office, he walked briskly down the dark hall. Yes, he'd go to Helsey Park and he'd find Allinton. But before he did anything as an agent of the Ramparts, he would first speak to Allinton as a friend and discover what his story was.

There had to be some other reason why a respected ex-agent would suddenly steal three rare gemstones.

Chapter Three

Mr. Allinton alighted from the coach in front of the magnificent facade of Helsey Park, the main residence of Lord Meynhill. The last time he'd been here, the yellowed stones of the buildings had been covered with ivy, but for the birthday celebration, all offending tendrils had been removed and the windows shone.

Lord Meynhill himself descended the front steps to greet him. "Good morning, Mr. Allinton. I have not seen you for many years. You are looking quite well, I am glad to see."

Allinton shook the man's hand, not too hard, since Lord Meynhill's grip was gentle. "I am well. You also look to be in fine fettle."

His smile was self-depricating. "Aside from a little ache in my knee, nothing of concern. How is your mother?"

"Also complaining of a little ache in her knee."

Lord Meynhill chuckled, which made his blue eyes shine. The slim man always had a soft, amiable expression that put everyone around him at ease. "My mother was very disappointed when her dear friend Marcus wrote his regrets for our celebration, but then to receive word that you would take his place was quite as delightful. I had not realized that you were related to the Naylor family."

"Marcus is my distant uncle," Allinton replied.

"If I had known, I might have given you a handicap when we

played cards at White's." Lord Meynhill winked.

"I would have refused you, and then later regretted it, my lord."

"I doubt it. A smart young man like yourself? You were married a few years ago, I believe."

They continued chatting for a few minutes, and Allinton knew his host had other duties, so he quickly asked, "I was hoping for a tour of your home, my lord. My mother mentioned that you had a very fine scroll from the 15th century, I believe."

"Ah, yes, the scroll I bought for a song on my Grand Tour. Goodness, that was decades ago." Lord Meynhill consulted his fine filigree pocket watch. "I have a little time now. Shall I show it to you?"

Allinton smiled. "By all means, my lord."

Chapter Four

The party of guests staying at Glencowe Castle reminded Sol of a herd of cattle. Slow to move, stubborn when it pleased them, wandering off in random directions when something caught their eye.

Sol happened to be standing next to the current Lord Wynwood on the grand staircase of his home as his house party guests milled about in the foyer below them, donning wraps and sending servants to bedrooms for forgotten articles. Lord Wynwood gave a barely audible sigh, then turned guiltily to Sol.

He smiled at the peer. "Just so, my lord."

Newland Glencowe, the 9th Viscount Wynwood, was perhaps ten years younger than himself and Laura, Lady Wynwood, but his face reminded Sol of Laura's deceased husband—a long nose, sharp chin, slightly sagging jaws despite his youth, as well as a prematurely receding hairline of ash-brown curls. Unlike the previous Lord Wynwood, his eyes were a warm brown instead of flint-gray, and without the cruelty lurking behind his gaze that always put Sol's back up.

"I must thank you again for allowing me to stay at your home at such short notice," Sol said.

The man waved a graceful hand. "As you can see, there are ample guests for this weekend, and one more is no strain."

"It was quite a feat for Lady Meynhill to arrange for the two other homes in the area to house her party guests. Did she threaten you with extraordinarily clumsy dance partners at her ball?"

Lord Wynwood chuckled. "Mr. Carver and I were glad to accommodate her. She is an excellent neighbor and her sixtieth birthday is worthy of a grand fete."

Privately Sol was surprised any woman would admit to her age, but it seemed acceptable if it gave her the excuse to throw the party of the year.

He joined Lord Wynwood in attempting to herd his guests to the waiting carriages that would take them to Helsey Park for a Venetian breakfast (regardless of the fact it was scheduled to start at noon) to open the weekend of festivities. But just before leaving the foyer, Laura's mother, Mrs. Cambrook, cried, "Oh! I've left my favorite Norwich shawl in my bedroom."

Trying not to grit his teeth, Sol said promptly, "I shall be happy to fetch it for you, ma'am." He would be riding in the carriage with Laura and her mother, so the sooner she had her shawl, the sooner they would leave.

However, before he turned to head upstairs to the guest bedrooms, he caught an intent look from Laura, her golden-brown eyes narrowing, and the pit of his stomach jumped. She could always read his moods, and she had most definitely realized he was impatient for some reason.

The shawl retrieved, Sol finally squeezed into a carriage with Laura, her mother, and Laura's cousin, Mrs. Edson.

"I didn't see you at breakfast this morning," Mrs. Edson said to Mrs. Cambrook. "It has been so long since I've seen you, Aunt, and I was hoping to have a long coze."

"I eat very little in the morning these days. I had tea and toast in my bedroom," she replied.

"You missed a delicious breakfast, Mama," Laura said. "Wynwood sets a sumptuous sideboard."

"He does indeed!" Mrs. Edson grinned. "I am ever so grateful to Lord Wynwood for allowing us to stay with him, though we are not directly related. However did you convince him?"

"He had agreed to house some of Lady Meynhill's guests, and he asked to house my family since we are not strangers to him," Laura said.

"It was still very gracious of him," Mrs. Edson said. "Georgina is in alt over her bedroom, despite complaining that she must share with her younger sister."

"Are you satisfied with your room, Mama?" Laura asked her mother.

"It is lovely. I must confess that although Nanette is my friend, Helsey Park is terribly drafty. Glencowe Castle is much more comfortable."

Sol bit back a smile. Mrs. Cambrook's bluntly delivered opinions reminded him of Laura. She also gave him a glimpse of what Laura might look like in twenty years, her smile lined but wide, her straight hair more silver than blonde, but thick and glossy. Mrs. Edson, Laura's cousin on her father's side, apparently looked more like the Cambrooks with her brown curly hair and blue-gray eyes.

"Oh, yes, Father used to tell us clankers about ice forming on the stairs in Helsey Park," Mrs. Edson said.

"They weren't stories, dear," Mrs. Cambrook said. "One Christmas, we did indeed have ice on the stairs to the gallery, and one of the maids slipped and fell."

Mrs. Cambrook told stories for the rest of the ride. She, Laura's deceased father, and his older brother had been friends with Lady Meynhill for many years, and so they had naturally been invited to the birthday party. Mrs. Edson and her two daughters had helped her father with the long journey from his home while Laura accompanied her mother.

Sol listened with only half an ear as they drew nearer to Helsey Park. He had realized that he was working as an agent for the first time in years. He had become used to telling agents what to do and where to go, but now he was the one doing and going.

He fought down an irrational surge of nervousness. This wasn't his first mission. While he might be rusty, he was still a competent agent, and he had a clear objective today—to find and talk to Allinton, who was certain to be at the breakfast.

Despite their tardiness, the group from Glencowe Castle was not the cause of the breakfast's late start. The party from Mr. Carver's home had not yet arrived.

The guests milled about on the lawn where tables and chairs had been set up. He helped Mrs. Cambrook to a chair, and he glanced around to see if he could spot Allinton. However, the area directly around him was too packed for him to see very far. He judged there to be at least sixty people, without counting those yet to arrive.

He turned to find Laura's gaze on him. He could feel a flush start at his neck and struggled to control himself. The woman was far too perceptive. He used to be more discreet in his actions, but years away from active work had made him sloppy.

He reminded himself of the mindset he used to have as an active agent. Observant eyes. Controlled facial features. A voice neither too loud nor too soft so that he would not draw attention to himself.

He had trained his agents by example. He may not have worked in the field for many years, but he could remember how to be stealthy, suave, and unobtrusive.

He smiled down at Mrs. Cambrook. "Might I fetch you something to drink? A cup of tea?"

"Yes, thank you, Mr. Drydale."

Her voice was very polite, as she always was when addressing him. Laura had confided to him once that her mother disliked their friendship after Wynwood died, because she feared Sol would attempt to woo her daughter. He was wealthy but not titled, a gentleman farmer and far below the social status of a daughter of the Cambrook family.

The irony was that he himself would never make their friendship more than purely platonic. He had too many secrets he kept from her, which would hurt her if she knew. And he also knew—or at least guessed—far more about her marriage to Wynwood than she probably wanted him to know.

Sol wove his way through the guests, taking a roundabout path to a table on the far end. He searched for Allinton's pale-colored hair and erect carriage but did not see him.

"Is that you, Mr. Drydale? I had no idea I would see you here!" A hearty voice interrupted his search, and he turned to see Mr. Jardine, an avid chess player from Sol's club—the outer portion, the Ivory Ramparts. Mr. Jardine didn't know about the more secretive department that worked behind those walls.

"An unexpected pleasure to see you, sir." Sol bowed to the older gentleman. "You are acquainted with Lady Meynhill?"

"Yes, she and my wife are childhood friends. And you?"

"In truth, I am an interloper," Sol said with a smile. "I came escorting Mrs. Cambrook and her daughter, Lady Wynwood." He had felt almost guilty that it had been so easy to convince Laura to allow him to join them. He had mentioned his sister-in-law's niece again trying to trap him into marriage and the need to leave town for a few days, and she had been more than pleased to accept his escort.

However, after seeing his distracted behavior, she might be regretting her kindness to him.

At that moment, he saw a swift movement behind Mr. Jardine, a familiar stiff set of shoulders, ash-blond hair cut shorter than was fashionable atop a head tilted at that forward angle, as if he were constantly moving forward.

"I do beg your pardon, sir," Sol said, "but I must fetch Mrs. Cambrook some tea. I hope to speak more at length with you during the weekend, however."

"Of course, of course. You seem unusually eager to please the Lady Wynwood's mother, eh?" Mr. Jardine gave him a wink.

Sol responded with a bland smile, bowed, and left him.

He wove through the crowd, his eyes scanning where he'd seen that familiar figure. And then he saw another glimpse.

His pace quickened, but he kept his movements smooth, and hopefully less noticeable by his quarry. He kept the back of the man's head in sight even as he ducked behind groups of people, trying to remain hidden.

He failed.

He knew exactly when Allinton spotted him. They didn't lock eyes or anything dramatic, but in between the time it took for Sol to pass behind two chatting groups of people, Allinton's actions suddenly changed. His direction sharply angled, his head seemed to lean forward even more, and he most definitely increased his walking speed.

Sol hissed in frustration and hurried after him, but he wasn't going to catch up before he reached one of the side doors into the manor house.

There was a sudden cry, and a few feet away from Allinton, an older woman touched her hand to her face, then staggered and fell.

Allinton spotted her, also. A girl perhaps twelve or thirteen years old stood nearby chatting to other girls, but she saw her and came to her side, helping the woman to sit up. Sol recognized her as Laura's cousin's daughter, Georgina Edson. Allinton's pace slackened.

And then he veered from his clear shot to the manor house in order to kneel beside the old woman.

"Mrs. Fairbanks, are you ill?" he asked.

"Oh, bless you, Stewart. I simply felt a touch of dizziness."

"Mrs. Fairbanks, you should lie down inside," Miss Edson said.

"Perhaps you are right, Georgina. Please help me to my feet."

"I'll do that." Mr. Allinton reached around the old woman with one arm while holding her hand with the other and helped her stand shakily on her feet. "Why don't I help you to the house, Mrs. Fairbanks?"

"Oh, no, you should enjoy yourself out here, Stewart, rather than playing nanny to an old lady."

"Don't be ridiculous, Mrs. Fairbanks. It isn't a bother at all."

Allinton didn't look in Sol's direction, but he knew he was aware of him as Sol approached. Allinton would have made it into the labyrinthine halls of the manor and likely would have eluded Sol if he hadn't stopped to help Mrs. Fairbanks.

He hadn't realized until this moment how tense he had been, uncertain if Allinton had changed, but he hadn't. This was the same young man he'd known, with whom he'd spent a weekend at his hunting lodge helping to improve his firing aim, whom he'd trained in how to lose a man tailing him by chasing him all over London's streets, with whom he'd talked about anything and everything during the long hours of waiting for a suspicious person they were following to emerge from a gaming hall or brothel.

He only wanted to speak to him. He wasn't about to bring him in without hearing his side of this story. But he didn't know how to get that across to him with these people all around them, who knew nothing of the department.

He tried to convey his intentions as he approached cautiously and said, "Allinton. It's very good to see you."

Allinton smiled at Sol, but it didn't reach his blue eyes. "Mr. Drydale, what a surprise."

"Is this a friend of yours, Stewart?" the old woman asked.

Stewart made the introductions, although he seemed reluctant to do so. He was about to introduce the young girl, who was following behind them a few paces, but Sol forestalled him. "Miss Georgina Edson and I are both staying at Glencowe Castle."

"You should stay here and catch up with Mr. Drydale," Mrs. Fairbanks said. "I can manage on my own."

"I wouldn't dream of doing any such thing, Mrs. Fairbanks," Allinton said firmly. "'Twould be like abandoning a young lady I had asked to dance. You wouldn't wish to leave me on the ballroom floor, would you, ma'am?"

She laughed and patted his arm where she was leaning heavily. "Such a silly boy. These old legs haven't danced in years."

Allinton looked at Sol. "I mustn't keep you, Mr. Drydale. I shall find another opportunity to chat with you during the weekend."

That was an outright lie. Allinton would be gone as soon as he accomplished whatever he intended to do here.

Miss Edson spoke up. "If you'd like, I can take Mrs. Fairbanks back to the house."

"We are quite comfortable, Mrs. Fairbanks and I," Allinton said with false heartiness. "You may return to your friends, if you wish."

"Oh," Miss Edson said airily, "they're only talking about things like dresses and things. It's quite boring."

Yes, Miss Edson was definitely a Cambrook.

Sol said, "Why don't I walk with you and Mrs. Fairbanks? We can walk back to the party." He smiled down at Mrs. Fairbanks and offered her his arm.

"Oh my," Mrs. Fairbanks twittered. "Two gallant swains, one on each arm. I am so spoiled."

She began reminiscing about other garden parties she had attended at Helsey Park, before Lord Meynhill's late father had been awarded the earldom, and while Allinton appeared to be listening to her, there was a tightness around his eyes and a stiffness to his face that told Sol he was feeling trapped and desperate to escape.

What was he doing, and why? If he would only explain it to

Sol, he could help him.

They had nearly reached the house when the door opened and a woman about Sol's age exited and spotted them. "Mother! Are you well?"

"Just a little dizziness, my dear."

"I shall help you to your room. Thank you, gentlemen." She nodded to the two men and took her mother's arm, steering her inside.

"Perhaps we could find a quiet place to chat?" Sol tried to keep his voice light, unthreatening.

"I'm afraid I'm quite busy, sir. If you would excuse me …"

Sol grabbed his arm. "Allinton, I only desire to talk."

He looked down at Sol's hand. "You aren't acting like a man who only desires to talk."

Sol's grip tightened. He couldn't deny that, and he couldn't simply release his arm, but he also wanted an opportunity to speak frankly with him.

Then the man's intelligent eyes did a quick scan of the people around them, and he said in a loud voice, "I say, sir, apologize for what you just said about Mr. Harwell!"

Heads turned in their direction, but the heads that moved fastest belonged to a group of three young men nearby, one of whom had stiff red-brown hair that stuck up in all directions. His face turned almost as red as his hair as he strode quickly toward them. "What's going on?"

Allinton feigned surprise. "Oh! Mr. Harwell, I didn't realize you were right there."

Mr. Harwell glared at Sol but spoke to Allinton. "What did he say about me?"

"Oh, well …" Allinton's acting was so good that he looked like he was truly trying to backpedal. "Nothing so terrible, now that I think on it. He said your hair reminded him of a strawberry trifle, which is really quite delicious—"

"You have some gall, you wrinkly old man!" Mr. Harwell

stepped even closer to Sol so that he was standing nose to nose. The young man was a little taller than he was, so Sol found himself staring up into angry hazel eyes.

"I said no such thing," Sol retorted.

"Now, Mr. Harwell," Allinton said, shaking off Sol's hand on his arm, "what he said was a bit insulting, but if you would simply *calm down* ..."

Those were apparently oft-heard admonitions for the young man, whose face turned a darker shade of red. "I'd like to see you remain calm when a knave has insulted my family's heritage!"

Allinton was backing away even as Mr. Harwell's two friends moved closer to flank him, so that Sol had to face three pairs of indignant eyes. In half a second, Allinton was moving through the crowd away from them.

Sol worked to tamp down his frustration, lest they make his words and actions curt. He adopted a humble, submissive mien and said, "I beg your pardon, won't happen again," just before he tried to sidestep Mr. Harwell to chase after Allinton.

He hadn't thought about how a hot-headed young man who'd apparently been insulted on a very sensitive topic would respond, regardless of the repentance of the sinner. Mr. Harwell grabbed at Sol's arm. "Do you dare to ignore me?"

Allinton would disappear from view in a moment. Sol expertly twisted his arm and gripped Mr. Harwell's wrist, forcing his fingers to open.

With the speed and quick reflexes of youth, Mr. Harwell swung wildly at Sol with his other hand.

Sol released the young man's wrist even as he blocked the blow. Mr. Harwell punched again, this time with his dominant hand, and Sol again blocked it. Sol drew his arm back for a quick jab to the young man's chin—something to daze him, as opposed to knocking him senseless—when his elbow struck something soft, and there was an even softer cry of pain.

He aborted his blow and twisted around to see whom he had assaulted.

And so he didn't see Mr. Harwell's next blow, which glanced off the back of his skull near his ear. Luckily it was an amateur strike without much power or precision behind it, so he only felt a blunted pain rather than seeing stars.

However, the impact sent him toppling forward, and he tangled his much larger bulk in the limbs of someone young and slender. They hit the ground hard, and a young girl cried out again in pain.

He had been so certain he would remember how to be stealthy, suave, and unobtrusive.

He had failed spectacularly at all three.

Even someone who didn't know Sol as well as Laura did would notice that he was acting strangely.

In fact, it was almost as though he were attempting to be *stealthy*. Inwardly, she rolled her eyes at that.

On the day he'd asked to join her for the birthday celebration, she had unfortunately been distracted with small household emergencies she needed to solve before leaving town. She knew both Lady Meynhill and Lord Wynwood would not mind an extra guest, although she had sent off quick notes to inquire.

The excuse he'd given to her had been the same as this past Christmas, and at that time Sol had been genuinely desperate to avoid his sister-in-law's machinations to throw him into company with her niece—or was it her cousin?

Sol was still handsome even at forty, with intelligent hazel eyes and thick, wavy hair still dark brown with only a few strands of silver. He had been extricating himself from interested women for many years, but it was more difficult with his brother's widow, especially when her tactics bordered on entrapping him rather than simply orchestrating situations that might encourage a possible marriage.

So she hadn't questioned his desire to join her and conveniently leave town for the weekend. However, she should have paid more attention when he'd asked her, because it was becoming apparent to her that he had another agenda in coming to Helsey Park.

"Laura," her mother said plaintively, "Mr. Drydale is very long in fetching my tea."

Laura rose from her seat with firm determination. "Quite right." She flagged down a passing servant and sent him for tea for her mother, which he did with alacrity. Then she made her excuses and went in search of Sol.

She eventually saw him moving through the crowd, heading in the direction of the manor house, and his eyes seemed very intent on someone ahead of him. Laura followed at a more sedate pace, but at an angle so she could better see whom he seemed to be following.

She recognized Mr. Allinton after only a moment's thought to try to remember his name. The way Sol chased him—and the way Mr. Allinton appeared to be trying to flee from Sol—was very odd because she recalled that they had been good friends several years ago.

She also remembered Mr. Allinton because she had heard his name recently, from two different friends in town. Mrs. Oldfield had attended the Newton soiree two or three weeks ago, and in passing, she remarked upon her surprise upon catching a glimpse of Mr. Allinton across the room. Last she had heard, he was rusticating in the country with his bride and newborn son.

Lady Treslove had been telling Laura about the Russby ball, and she'd listed in detail everyone she'd seen. She had also been surprised to see Mr. Allinton and had wished she had been able to speak to him about his new family.

Laura herself had attended the Holmendale ball that had

ended in such disaster, and she recalled seeing Mr. Allinton accompanying the Isherwoods from the foyer and climbing into their carriage. At the time, she hadn't remembered his name but he had looked familiar to her.

Mrs. Oldfield had not attended the Russby ball, and Lady Treslove had not been to the Newton soiree. Mrs. Oldfield had not been invited to the Holmendale ball, and Lady Treslove had been bitterly disappointed that her daughter had caused them to be late so that they arrived after the theft had been discovered and their carriage was turned away.

A connection she hadn't made was between Mr. Allinton and the thefts at those three events.

The theft of the Pennleigh Sapphire at the Newton soiree was not known by many people, because it had been discovered only after the guests had gone home, but Laura had heard a few friends gossiping about it. Mrs. Oldfield, who had attended the event, had not known about it when she was chatting with Laura the day after.

The theft of the Virgilius Emerald at the Russby ball was also not spread about, but she was friends with Lady Russby and had been a comforting shoulder for her to cry upon at the loss of the gemstone.

However, everyone knew about the stolen Isadora Diamond from the Holmendale ball. But only about half of the invited guests had arrived before the party was cancelled, so Laura was one of the few who had witnessed the upheaval in the house.

And quite possibly one of the few who had seen Mr. Allinton at the ball.

And now Sol was following Mr. Allinton.

She had difficulty believing Mr. Allinton would steal priceless gemstones. Also, each safe box had been opened without the use of the key, an amazing feat. Would someone like Mr. Allinton have a unique skill like that?

Also, Lord Meynhill did not collect gemstones. As far as she knew, he was not a connoisseur of art or jewels or anything of the sort, although the family had gathered a respectable collection of fine art pieces over the decades. However, they did not own anything extraordinary like the three famous gemstones that had been taken.

She kept herself at a distance, so she was too far away to rush in to help when Mrs. Fairbanks collapsed. However, it was curious that Mr. Allinton, despite clearly attempting to elude Sol's pursuit, had yet swerved from his path to help the old woman, even though it allowed Sol to catch up to him. His concern for Mrs. Fairbanks was quite genuine, as far as Laura could tell, and she was usually right about her judgments in that area.

Would a man like that really commit such thefts?

She continued to keep her distance, watching the players and wondering to herself why it intrigued her. She didn't know if Sol wanted to speak to Mr. Allinton about the thefts or about something else, but it was none of her concern. So why was she spying on them? She even deftly avoided the notice of some of her friends and acquaintances who were milling around the lawn so that no one would distract her from her task.

And then there had been the fracas with Mr. Harwell, an easily excitable young man. She almost felt sorry for Sol, and noted Mr. Allinton's clever ruse to escape from him.

She then realized that she was in a position to follow Mr. Allinton herself, and she was torn as to whether she ought to or not. This was not her affair, and yet she had seen so much of this secret performance.

Her decision was made for her when Mr. Harwell's fists began flying. She immediately noticed Georgina, her cousin's daughter, standing too closely behind Sol.

His elbow knocked hard into Georgina's collarbone, and she jerked into a curled motion with a cry. Sol immediately turned toward her, but Mr. Harwell continued punching and caught Sol on the back of the head. He went tumbling down, directly on top of Georgina.

Sol was not an overly large man, and he kept himself very fit, but he was several stone heavier than the young girl, and she had already been injured by his accidentally driven elbow. Laura picked up her skirts, disregarding propriety, and rushed toward them.

Mr. Allinton was hurrying toward her, away from the conflict. But then something very strange happened.

A maid deliberately stepped in front of Mr. Allinton. Irritation crossed his face, and Laura would have expected him to simply shove the maid aside in his haste to escape. But his pace faltered, and he tried to move around the woman.

And then the maid tripped him.

It was just as deliberate as when she stepped in front of him. However, she put her hand to her mouth and cried, "Oh!" in surprise as Mr. Allinton fell. She then went to her knees next to him.

Except that instead of trying to help him up, she seemed to be attempting to *hold him down*.

Laura was still heading toward Georgina and Sol, and Allinton and the maid were in her path, so she saw this quite clearly. The maid grabbed Mr. Allinton's arm, then his leg, and seemed to be almost pushing him down even as he was trying to scramble away.

He looked directly at the maid and glared at her, but otherwise did not respond to her strange behavior. Nor did he shove her away or use his strength violently upon her, but simply attempted to escape.

The attention of most of the guests was caught by the fisticuffs between Sol and Mr. Harwell, so only a few noticed Mr. Allinton's fall. An older gentleman, perhaps a decade older than Sol and dressed like a servant, approached the maid and Mr. Allinton. But rather than the confusion or consternation she would expect from a servant, he regarded the struggle calmly. In fact, he seemed intent upon helping the maid.

"Allinton! Are you hurt?" Lord Meynhill approached and waved away the maid, who obeyed reluctantly. He offered a hand to Mr. Allinton to help him to his feet. "What happened?"

"My own clumsy feet," he replied without even a glance at the maid. "I was distracted by Mr. Harwell's dispute and was attempting to walk and turn around to look at the same time."

"I came this direction because of the younger Harwell, but it looks as though his father has arrived to take him in hand."

Indeed, an older gentleman with red locks more faded than his son's had come up behind the boy, looking furious.

Laura passed Mr. Allinton and Lord Meynhill with an abbreviated curtsey, then hurried to Georgina, still on the ground. Sol had risen to his feet, clearly conscious-stricken as he looked down at the girl.

"Shall I carry you into the house?" he was asking her as Laura approached.

She knelt beside Georgina, who had sat up but was curled in on herself, her face twisted in pain. "Where does it hurt, dear?"

"It hurts to move my arm." The girl's other hand covered the front of her shoulder, near her collarbone.

"Sol, take her other side and help her to her feet. Gently ..."

He immediately obliged, and his grip on the girl was gentle, but she winced and went pale as she stood. He kept his arm around her, steadying her.

"Can you walk?"

Georgina bit her lip and nodded, then suddenly noticed everyone staring at her, and went beet red.

Sol supported her as they walked into the house, and Lady Meynhill personally directed them to a bedroom they could use. She also sent a servant to call for the local doctor.

Sol bowed deeply to his hostess. "I sincerely apologize for the disturbance at your party."

"Do not blame yourself too much, Mr. Drydale. Welch Harwell fights with someone at nearly every gathering he attends."

"As one older and wiser, I should not have allowed myself to become involved."

"You are not yet that old." She smiled at him. "It may simply prove you still have a spring in your step, even at your age."

Sol bowed again in apology as she left the bedroom, but outside the doorway she stopped as Laura's cousin Georgeanne arrived, and spoke briefly to her. Georgeanne curtseyed to Lady Meynhill, then came inside with concern for her daughter.

Laura lost track of Sol after that, since she was busy helping her cousin to care for Georgina. The doctor came sooner than expected and pronounced her to have a dislocated collarbone. When he reset it, Georgina passed out from the pain.

While Georgeanne talked quietly with the doctor, Laura fussed over things that didn't need fussing over as she watched over the unconscious Georgina. Finally she forced herself to stop fluttering about and collapsed in a chair next to the bed.

A part of her didn't want to think about what she'd just seen at the Venetian breakfast. Sol had obviously come to the Meynhill birthday celebration to speak to Mr. Allinton, or perhaps even detain him somehow, since Sol's attitude seemed rather hard and urgent.

She would have supposed his reasons were personal, if not for the curious coincidence of the gemstone thefts, and the maid.

The maid had been actively helping Sol. Which meant she knew what his agenda was, and they were intent upon capturing Mr. Allinton. Laura was even willing to suspect the older servant who approached the maid and Mr. Allinton had also been involved somehow.

In a large party like this, it would be simple to slip in dressed as a maid and footman. She had no evidence they were in disguise, but the maid's actions were too suspicious.

And if the woman was in disguise, and helping Sol, then there was something else afoot here.

Sol had always kept his "other" life secret. She suspected, but she never asked him any questions.

But now, had he brought his "other" life into the midst of this party? Involving her family, no less? It concerned her.

She also had to admit to herself that she was in high dudgeon at the fact that he had used her in order to gain access to the party, even if his work was important for the good of the country.

She didn't know how long Sol had been serving his government in this capacity, but because of his friendship with Mr. Allinton, she wondered if he also was involved in the same work. But if so, why was there the strange connection between him and the three thefts? Was Sol pursuing him for that reason?

Sol, she was certain, came to the party to apprehend Mr. Allinton, but why had Mr. Allinton come? And he had not snuck into the party, but he was invited, and a room made up for him at Helsey Park. She did not think he attached himself to another party of invited guests, as Sol had done, because Lord Meynhill had known him. Was he a good friend of the family, and he would naturally come to celebrate Lady Meynhill's birthday? Or had he some other reason?

And the curious part about all of it was that Lord Meynhill had no gemstones to steal. As far as she knew, he had no one piece of extraordinary value in his home.

Regardless, she didn't wish Mr. Allinton to steal anything from Lady Meynhill or her son. Because of her mother's friendship with Nanette Howey, Laura had become close to the family. After her marriage to Wynwood, since his principle seat was so near to Helsey Park, she had always made sure to visit Lady Meynhill when they took up residence at Glencowe Castle. After Wynwood died and the title passed to his cousin Newland

Glencowe, the current Lord Wynwood, Laura had not visited Lady Meynhill as often, but she still corresponded with her and visited whenever family obligations brought her back to the area.

Was she trying to give herself permission to become involved in all this? She didn't know whether she should laugh or sigh at herself.

There were some things she knew for a certainty: Sol would not tell her anything if she asked him, she was feeling a burning fire in her chest at the knowledge that he had used her, and she was even more upset that he had brought his work here and it had caused injury, albeit indirectly, to her family, Georgina.

And even if Sol weren't here, she would want to protect the Howey family.

Georgina stirred and saw Laura sitting nearby.

"How are you feeling, darling?"

"I feel ..." The girl winced. "... perfectly awful." She looked at Laura and her brows knit. "You look perfectly awful too, Cousin Laura."

Laura's eyebrows rose.

"I mean ..." Georgina bit her lip. "You always look so calm and controlled, but right now you look like you'd like to slap someone."

Laura laughed, a deep belly laugh, although she admitted there might have been a slightly higher-pitched edge of temper to her voice. "You are very perceptive, just like a Cambrook."

"I do hope you won't hurt anyone." Georgina gave a small smile. "And I'm also an Edson, so that means I'm even more perceptive, right?"

"It means you're probably wiser than all of us crazy old ladies."

"Aw, don't say that, Cousin Laura. You're not old." She grinned.

"No comment about the 'crazy,' I see."

"Mama taught me never to tell a lie."

She was not far off on the crazy part. Laura was contemplating something she never would have considered if Sol had not brought his "other" life so directly into hers. She would do everything she could to protect her family.

Even as she thought that, an insidious voice inside of her whispered, *Doing all you can now won't change the one time you failed.*

Her thoughts grew dark for a moment, but then she recalled what she had read in her Bible that morning in the book of Psalms:

He brought me up also out of an horrible pit, out of the miry clay,

and set my feet upon a rock, and established my goings.

And he hath put a new song in my mouth,

even praise unto our God: many shall see it, and fear, and shall trust in the LORD.

The Lord God had lifted her up, so she could no longer beat herself down.

She knew what she had to do. It didn't matter that she didn't have the kind of experience and training that Sol must have had, or that maid-who-wasn't-a-maid.

However, she had her own secret abilities she could employ, and an event like this was the perfect place for her to use them.

Chapter Five

Sol looked for Allinton again, however, he discovered that the man had volunteered to escort Mrs. Fairbanks and her daughter to visit a relative in the area, and they had left in a carriage soon after the Venetian breakfast ended.

Lord Meynhill's safe was in the master's study, according to the information Sir Derrick had given to him, so he thought to position himself nearby in the event Allinton returned early. However, Lord Meynhill had sequestered himself in his study with his steward that afternoon. Sol also discovered that a good vantage point to watch the study did not exist unless he wanted to crouch down in a closet across the hallway and possibly frighten and scandalize the butler.

He wanted to avoid being trapped in a carriage with Laura, who likely had questions for him regarding his behavior, and so he had opted to stay behind at Helsey Park rather than returning to Glencowe Castle, only to find that she had remained behind as well, accompanying her mother in a visit to Lady Meynhill. He felt that avoiding her was still his best plan, so he spent one or two fruitless hours speaking to servants about Allinton, then finally retreated in sour spirits to a small sitting room, uncomfortably hot despite the cool spring weather and decorated in pinks and reds and lace that was an affront to his manliness. However, it was empty and out of the way, and therefore served his purpose. He paced restlessly in front of the small windows of the corner room until the afternoon had advanced, waiting.

There was a knock at the door, and a maid entered carrying a tray with tea and cakes. As she set it on the table next to the chair in front of the fireplace, Sol asked, "Well? What did you find?"

The young woman, Lena Penrose, turned to him with a perfect mask of confusion. "I beg your pardon, sir? I don't understand."

"The room is secure. There's a linen closet on one side and a creaking servants' stairwell on the other."

"Which you checked in the last ten minutes?" Her cheeky tone somehow reminded him of Laura, but she was right. According to the file Sir Derrick had given to him on Miss Penrose, she had been the victim of some unusual situation and had been an agent for almost eight years, since she was eighteen years old. She was trained by Mr. Wilfrid Neybridge, a longtime agent who had worked in France during the French Revolutionary War, just as Sol had, although they had never worked on a mission together until now.

Sol checked the stairwell while Miss Penrose checked the linen closet. Since it was a corner room, there was little possibility of being overheard.

"Sir, won't you sit down?" Miss Penrose gestured to seat in front of the fireplace, next to the table where she had laid the tray.

Sol realized he was being too irritable, but it was not with the two agents Sir Derrick had sent to work with him. He was frustrated with himself, and frustrated that Allinton had gotten away.

There was an itching in his gut that told him that Allinton would act soon, and he was running out of time. It gave his words a sharpness as he asked, "Where is ... David?" Good

Lord, Sol nearly forgot to call Mr. Neybridge by his alias, which all agents were instructed to do when on a mission in order to protect their true identities. He'd been out of the game for too long.

"Following Mr. Allinton, of course," she said.

He should have known that. On the continent, Mr. Neybridge had been extraordinarily skilled at disguises and remaining unobserved, so of course he would be the one to shadow Mr. Allinton on his visit with Mrs. Fairbanks.

"I tried discovering which room in Helsey Park belonged to Allinton, but apparently some guests had switched rooms, and the Manor house has over fifty guest rooms." He settled in the chair with a little more force than was needed.

She poured tea, looking for all the world like the maid she appeared to be. "David and I had no difficulties slipping into the garden party and posing as two more of the other temporarily hired help. I discovered which room is Mr. Allinton's, but he is sharing with another gentleman, so David was unable to go forward with our original plan for him to wait for him inside his room."

"He probably deliberately arranged to share a room with another in order to thwart any efforts to ambush him in his bedroom." Sol sipped morosely at the tea that Miss Penrose had poured for him.

"After the, err, accident," Miss Penrose said, coloring slightly at mention of Sol's social gaffe, "I snuck into the house and searched Mr. Allinton's room while David followed him around at the Venetian breakfast. He was never alone," she added, "in the event you were about to ask."

"Allinton wouldn't be that careless," Sol grumbled.

"I found nothing unusual in his room," Miss Penrose said, "however, while I was there, a note was slipped under the door."

Sol leaned forward in his seat. "Who delivered the note? What did it say?"

"I rushed out of the room and found the pageboy who had delivered it. He said that one of the gentlemen guests at the Venetian breakfast asked him to deliver the message, but he didn't know the man's name. He was an older gentleman, but had no distinguishing features. He may not even have been invited to the party, since anyone dressed appropriately could pose as a guest," Miss Penrose said, gesturing toward her own servant's garb to illustrate the point.

Sol grunted in acknowledgment. "What did the note say?"

A furrow formed between Miss Penrose's brows. "When I returned to the bedroom after talking to the pageboy, the other gentleman who shared the room had arrived and discovered the note. He pocketed it, and according to David, he delivered it to Mr. Allinton at the party. I apologize, sir. If I'd been a little faster, I might have seen the note first."

Sol shook his head. "There was nothing you could have done about that."

She gave him a half-smile. "You are far kinder to me than David."

That was because Mr. Neybridge was her family—her distant cousin, to be exact. When he returned to England, he'd surprised everyone in the department when he'd taken her in to be a companion to his daughter, Dorothea.

"Sir, I feel we must bring in more agents," Miss Penrose said. "The party is too crowded for just the three of us to be able to capture him."

Sol shook his head. "I don't want to do that yet. More people will alarm Allinton. I don't want him to run, I want to talk to him first."

"I think it is obvious that he knows why you are here, sir, and he has no wish to speak to anyone from the department," Miss Penrose said in an even voice, attempting not to sound as though she were arguing against Sol.

"I think Allinton is still a good man, and that there is a

reason why he is doing this," Sol said. "He could have escaped me in the crowd, but he stopped to help Mrs. Fairbanks instead. It makes me believe that he is still the same man that I knew."

The furrow reappeared between Miss Penrose's brows. "When I first stepped in front of him, he could have simply shoved me aside, but he was polite to me even though I was clearly a maid. After I tripped him, and I was trying to keep him down, he knew I was an agent because he muttered, 'I should have known he wouldn't be alone.' Any other man might have slapped me or backhanded me, especially knowing that I wasn't an actual maid, but he didn't." Miss Penrose's gaze was clear, but there was a murky darkness behind them that spoke of past experience as she said, "I have experienced what truly selfish men are like, and Mr. Allinton isn't one of them. I agree with you, sir, but there is still the matter of the broken safes and the stolen gemstones, and the fact that he ran from you."

"He wouldn't steal those gemstones for profit," Sol said. "Someone is controlling him, somehow. Perhaps that was in the note that the pageboy delivered to his room. There is a deeper mystery here that we ought to try to solve first, before simply bringing Allinton in."

Miss Penrose nodded. "When he returns, what would you have us do?"

"Allinton won't get caught alone again or place himself where any one of us could seize him. He also knows now that you are not a true maid, and if he saw David approach to help you at the Venetian breakfast, he may already suspect that he is not a servant, either."

Miss Penrose tilted her head. "If I were him, I would be watchful for anyone following me, and I would take obscure ways to and from my bedroom. I would look for anyone who might be watching my room, and I would always enter the bedroom cautiously and be wary of a trap."

Sol nodded, impressed. Mr. Neybridge had trained her well.

"Allinton knows that I won't try to do anything to him with other people around."

"We can try to trap him with two of us. One can draw away whoever is with Mr. Allinton while you talk to him."

"However, I can't walk the hallways of Helsey Park all day with the maid or footman by my side. Allinton probably knows that, too."

"David suggested a pincer attack at the card party tonight. It must be something that Mr. Allinton will not suspect or be able to predict, something that he wouldn't think of."

"Or he may use the card party to make his move on the safe," Sol said. "Perhaps we should—"

He nearly jumped at the sharp knock at the door. He looked at Miss Penrose, but she was already busying herself at the tray, pouring him another cup of tea. "Come."

The door opened to reveal the butler, looking slightly flustered. "Mr. Drydale?"

"Yes."

"A note for you, sir." He handed it to Sol. "I apologize for the delay. We were told you were within the manor house, but not which room."

"It is nothing. Thank you."

The butler bowed and left.

Sol recognized the handwriting that wrote his name on the outside of the piece of paper. Curious, he opened it and read the contents.

He was not entirely certain how he ought to react. He stared down at the note.

"Sir," Miss Penrose said, and there was a twist at the corner of her mouth that indicated she was trying not to smile. "You look as if you swallowed a bug."

Allinton had had various jam tarts throughout his wild and

reckless childhood, but none seemed quite as sweet as those served by Mrs. Fairbanks's niece during their visit that afternoon. Or perhaps he enjoyed them so much because he had a looming sense of dread that his days of eating jam tarts would soon be over.

Mrs. Fairbanks teased him about it as he handed her down from the carriage in the front drive of Helsey Park. "With so many tarts in your stomach, you'll not have room for dinner, my boy."

"I always have room for dinner, Mrs. Fairbanks." He even managed a credible smile.

She laughed. "You're so like your father."

What would he say if he knew what his son was doing? Probably look at him with those sad brown eyes, which Stewart couldn't withstand for more than a minute before confessing everything to him.

He left the women on the landing toward the wing of the house where they were situated, then made as if to go to his own room, but instead returned to the ground floor.

During the Venetian breakfast, several ground floor rooms had been in use. The dining room had been used to hold trays of glasses and foods ready to be served, and the morning room as well as a small sitting room had been where the servants stored the extra outerwear of the guests who arrived from Glencowe Castle and Mr. Carver's home.

In addition, the library's double doors that opened directly into the garden had been left open so that guests arriving in the foyer could travel down the hallway and through the library and then directly into the garden, rather than walking around the house.

The master's study was not opened, but there were a great deal of guests and servants traversing the hallway outside. Later during the breakfast, a few young men had taken advantage of the billiards room that had been newly remodeled in the room next door to the study.

Allinton walked the hallway outside the study, peeking into the empty billiards room, and then continuing to the end of the hall. He turned down another corridor and walked past the library, checking inside both the library and the morning room next door to ascertain there was no one about.

He walked this route twice, which would have looked odd if anyone had been around to see him doing it. Then on the second route, he ducked into the library.

The late afternoon sun cast a golden light over the dark woods of the bookcases and the long table in the center of the room, highlighting motes of dust that hung in the air. The table stood slightly askew, since the servants had moved it aside to allow easy access to the double doors, and then moved it back after the party ended. Allinton paused at the doors, noting that they were open, but he left them that way. It would enable him to exit quickly if anyone (named Drydale) happened upon him.

He didn't blame Drydale for being here, for pursuing him. It was what he would have done. But he'd had to freeze his heart, and it had grown hard and numb.

In the far corner of the room, out of the light from the windows, stood a cabinet with glass doors, edged in brass fittings. There was an antique lock, easily broken, but Allinton had no need to do so. He reached up and behind the cabinet for the key that Lord Meynhill had retrieved when he showed Allinton the folio earlier yesterday.

He eased the door open slowly, his hands deft and delicate, so that there was only the barest squeak from the brass hinges. His hand reached inside the crack of the door and removed the folio in the blink of an eye.

He'd never intended to become a gentleman thief. He'd been recruited for the secret department that called itself the Ramparts when he'd been invalided home from the army. Wellington's words of praise had somehow reached Sir Derrick

Bayberry, and he offered Stewart the job. His first mission had been to return to France and retrieve a list of traitors on English soil, locked in a safebox. A man at the Ramparts had taught him the basics of breaking into the safe, but he'd discovered an unnatural knack to it, a feel in his hands.

He stared at the folio in his hands. He thought he'd left all this behind him when he retired. But after tonight, they would surely make the connection between himself and the thefts. Except that they would not be able to find him. He would have disappeared.

A sudden rattling at the doors made him tense for half a second. Then he quickly slipped the folio into the heavy pasteboard box he'd brought for it. He closed the cabinet door and pocketed the key, dropping the box to the carpet and sliding it into the shadows with his foot.

The doors opened and a woman peeked into the library, her blonde hair haloed in burnt orange light from behind her. She seemed to immediately look toward where he stood in front of the glass cabinet.

It was Lady Wynwood. She smiled when she saw him. "Hello, Mr. Allinton. I thought I saw you at the window."

Except that he had been careful not to pass in front of the window. Had she seen his shadow moving through the room? She would only have seen it if she'd been closely watching the windows.

"My lady, you were out in the garden?"

"You could say that."

She left the doors open as she walked into the room, and a light breeze chilled his skin. Or was it the memory of moments like these, being caught and needing to put on a calm, genial facade until he could escape? He'd had only a couple moments like that, and he had been able to keep his heart rate slow and steady in those times. Now, his heart slammed fast and hard.

And yet, she was simply a noblewoman. Average height,

widowed and no longer young, although still slim and with more smile lines than age wrinkles. What was it about her that made him so wary? She had breezed in like any other house party guest, and yet he somehow felt like prey being stalked.

To cover his unease, he moved to the lamp that sat on the table, but she waved her hand. "There is no need to light that for my sake."

The way she worded that was ... odd.

She continued, "I knew you would show up at the library. I'm so glad I was right."

He willed his muscles to remain loose and easy. "How did you know I'd be here?"

"I found out about the folio, Mr. Allinton." She smiled at him, and it only made him more unsettled.

"I beg your pardon—"

"Oh, you needn't deny it. And I could not stop you."

He did not answer her.

She walked around the table, which stood between himself and the door, but it wasn't an impossible obstacle. He should leave her, and yet something about her eyes and the way she walked toward him seemed to freeze him in place. As if a huge, invisible hand had wrapped around him.

"This afternoon, while my mother was chatting with Lady Meynhill, I had an interesting conversation with Lady Cliffton. Do you know her?"

"Only by acquaintance." His eyes darted to the open doors, then to the door to the hallway. Should he run? She couldn't stop him. But she could scream if she wanted. She hadn't said she wouldn't shout for someone to come.

"She is well known to love her jewelry." Lady Wynwood stopped only a few feet away from him. "Some call her ostentatious. I find some of her pieces dramatic, but on a whole, she has excellent taste."

"Were you thinking of buying jewelry?" Where was this story

going?

"Oh, no." She gave him an indulgent smile, like a mother to her son. "What most people don't realize is that she is also quite knowledgeable about gemstones."

He tried to remain relaxed, but he couldn't stop the muscle from jumping in his neck. Her eyes might have darted there and seen it, but she didn't react if she did.

"She had only heard of the theft of the Isadora Diamond, not the other stones, so she thought nothing of my questions when I asked her for more information about the diamond. I must admit, I was not as surprised to discover that the Isadora Diamond, the Pennleigh Sapphire, and the Virgilius Emerald are connected to each other. I do not believe in such things, but they are rumored to have mystical properties when they are brought together."

Mystical properties? Even he hadn't known that.

"When I first heard of the thefts, I had assumed the thief simply liked rare gems. But that isn't the case, is it?" She walked to the bookcase to his right, squinting at a bust that stood on an upper shelf.

"I wouldn't know, my lady. I had not heard that the other two were stolen."

She gave him a look of frank admiration. "You are quite believable. One of the best liars I have ever encountered."

Did she expect him to respond to that?

"Lady Cliffton also told me about a rare folio that are pages from an old journal in an ancient language and translated into Latin. It goes into detail about the three stones and how to use them. And coincidentally, it was bought by Lord Meynhill on his Grand Tour and resides in his library display case." She nodded to the cabinet behind him.

"Yes, Lord Meynhill showed it to me yesterday." He daren't bend down to pick up the box now. He tried to stop himself from leaning closer to the cabinet to block her view of the empty space where the folio had been.

"Lady Cliffton was rather more informed than I would have expected. She knew a handful of collectors who would want the stones and folio, but she said that none of them are wealthy enough to be able to hire thieves skilled enough to steal them. When I asked how she should know how much a good thief would cost, she turned quite red." Lady Wynwood laughed lightly. "She said that none of the collectors are very wealthy men, and it would cost a great deal of money to steal four items from four noble houses who have the best of security and protection."

"Yes. The theft of the diamond was quite brazen and would have been thought impossible by many."

"The folio, on the other hand, does not have any extraordinary intrinsic value. There are other folios older, and which contain more weighty or valuable writings."

She gave him another smile, and now that he was closer to her, even in the orange light from the windows, he could see that her smile was not cold, or arch, but warm and inviting, as if they were friends sharing a cup of tea. That smile somehow made him feel irrationally guilty to be following this course.

"So you see," she said, "I knew you were going to show up in the library."

The smile was still warm, but her words made his heart freeze.

She continued, "I suspected you would attempt for the folio quite soon, since Sol almost captured you earlier today. I also thought you might come here when the other guests were occupied with dressing for dinner, although you made a good show of attempting to allay suspicion by publicly promising to partner Mr. Harwell at the card party tonight. I don't think you convinced Sol you would be at the entertainment tonight, however."

She had started speaking in a slower, more measured cadence.

It made his brain feel sluggish. He no longer needed to come up with an excuse to leave. He should simply collect the folio and push past her.

He backed up a step and bent down to retrieve the box that held the folio. "This has been entertaining, my lady—"

"Hear me out," she entreated. "I won't stop you from leaving with that. I won't even shout for anyone to come."

He hesitated, but she seemed to be telling the truth, although he didn't understand why she would do that. Lady Wynwood had a reputation of being very religious, although he also recalled tales of her unconventional behavior and blunt tongue. She was very well-liked by most of society, and the fact she was a Cambrook ensured she received respect even from sticklers who might want to shun her for her refusal to adhere to the strict rules of society at times.

"I know why you didn't attempt for the folio at the Venetian breakfast," she said. "The library was thrown open for the guests to pass through. Sol probably had been convinced your aim was the safe in the study, and he likely assumed you didn't attempt the safe because the hallway outside the study was in use at that time, and then later the billiards room next door."

She stepped closer to him, and her eyes seemed to hold his. "But I don't understand why you didn't sneak down in the middle of the night to take the folio. Unless ..." Her eyes alighted. "Ah, I see. There would be a hue and cry once it was discovered to be missing, and Lord Meynhill would have all the rooms searched, including the guest rooms. If you wished to remain unsuspected, you wouldn't be able to simply abscond with the folio after you stole it. You would have to remain here and pretend to be one of the innocent guests."

He didn't know why he couldn't ignore her and shove her aside, rude as that would be. As before, he felt as though an invisible hand had closed around him, keeping him in place, and his mind felt fogged as her eyes bore into his.

"So it had to be this evening," she concluded. "Sol might have been fooled into thinking you wanted to enter the study, but I knew where you were going."

With effort, he shook off the strange numbness in his thoughts. "My lady—"

Suddenly, a sensation of a sharp touch to the back of his head. He didn't understand why his head jerked forward, because the blow hadn't felt too forceful ... but a second later, the pain exploded in the base of his skull, delayed like the thunder after the lightning.

Someone had come up behind him and hit him. Through the *doors she had left open.* And all her talk had been to hold his attention and turn his body away from the doors.

She's quite clever. Just like her reputation.

Strangely, his thoughts were calm as he fell to the floor. His sight had grown dark ... or perhaps that was because he had closed his eyes.

As his consciousness drifted away, he thought he heard her speaking to whoever had come up behind him (probably someone named Drydale).

"It took you long enough to respond to my note. I thought I'd need to start reciting my family tree before you finally snuck up on him."

Allinton sank into darkness.

Chapter Six

Sol stared at Laura, not certain if he wished to shake her or recruit her for the Ramparts. His mind went to other things he'd like to do to her, but shied away quickly. Lately it had been harder to battle his attraction and affection for her and adhere to the many reasons not to disrupt his good friendship with her.

Only at that moment did Miss Penrose appear through the doors, out of breath from running. Back in the Valentine colored room, he had handed her Laura's note and then run for the library.

In the note, Laura had succinctly laid out what she'd learned about Allinton's target—not the master's safe, but a folio in the library—and her belief that he would attempt the theft that very afternoon. She hadn't been able to find Sol, so she had written the note, outlining her intention to waylay Allinton with the help of her servants. If Sol received the note in time, he should enter the library through the outside double doors, which she would leave open for him.

He didn't want to admit it was a solid plan. When she entered the library, Allinton would be forced to pretend to be a normal guest, and she would distract him enough for her coachman to sneak up on him. When Sol had been running pell-mell toward the library's outer door, he had seen the large, hulking man posing as a gardener with a wheelbarrow outside the library and had taken his place to ambush Allinton.

Sol stared down at Allinton's limp form. Perhaps he should have attempted to restrain him rather than knocking him out, so that he could walk to another room in the house on his own two feet? But Sol reversed that regret quickly. Allinton would have found a way to escape if he had left him conscious.

"We can't simply carry him about the halls like this," he said. "But we can't speak to him with any privacy here."

"I have an idea, sir." Miss Penrose left quickly in a rustle of skirts.

Laura had bent to pick up a pasteboard box on the floor, carefully extracting the folio and returning it to the case, which he'd left open when Laura interrupted him. "Sol, please search his pockets. I believe I saw him slip the key inside when I entered the library."

As he bent to search for the key, she complained, "It took you long enough to get my note."

"You didn't give any instructions as to where I would be, so the butler had to search the house for me." In an extra pocket sewn into Allinton's jacket, Sol found a hard bulge and removed a cloth pouch with a gemstone.

"Well, since I hadn't been able to find you, I couldn't give him directions, could I? I would have thought you'd be in the billiards room or teasing the cook out of a seed cake."

"A seed cake? I'm hardly a child." Sol found two more gemstones as well as the key to the cabinet, which he handed to her with ill grace.

"Well, you are exceedingly sulky right now, probably because I discovered a piece of information you needed and helped you in your ... work." She was surprisingly delicate about his secret involvement in the government. He had suspected she knew, and yet she never said anything about it. She knew a great deal about the goings on of society, and yet she did not have the reputation of a gossip.

Her words made him angry, probably because she was too close to the truth. "I'm upset because you put yourself in danger. You had no idea what Allinton was capable of."

"I had Mr. Havner outside and the twins in the hallway."

"Your servants?" Granted, her coachman, Blake Havner, was a hulk of a man with fists larger than heads of cabbages, and her young pageboy and scullery maid had been street rats before she had rescued them from a child slavery auction.

"I asked them to position themselves near the doors in the event Mr. Allinton attempted to escape, or if he threatened me," Laura said.

"You were confronting a dangerous man. If he did threaten you, what would mere servants be able to do to a man trained like Allinton?" His worry for her was seeping through in the harshness of his tone.

"It was better than no one, especially when I worried that you hadn't yet received my note. It was either the twins or my maid, Aya, and the twins are much handier with their knives than she is."

"Their knives is not the point." He took a breath to try to calm himself. "You are a civilian, and you told other civilians about ... things which I would not wish to be bandied about."

She gave him a level glare. "They're my servants, Sol. I trusted them with my life. I can certainly trust them with your secrets."

Despite his jumbled frame of mind and his concern for her, he noted the odd past tense she used when she said she "trusted" her servants. He remembered reports he'd read about the former Lord Wynwood, the barely discernible bruises he'd seen peeking out around the edges of her gowns. As an agent, he should question her unwavering faith in her servants, but as her friend, he had no need to probe further.

Laura had collided headlong with the secret life he'd kept

from everyone he knew in society, and he didn't like it. He didn't want her even on the fringes of the dangerous things he had to investigate, the darker things he had to do.

There was no standard protocol for something like this, for someone unrelated to the Ramparts to force her way into a mission, especially when she had used her own unique skills to uncover what Allinton had been truly after, which was more than Sol had done. It made him feel like a man standing in a rowboat in choppy waters.

No, it made him irritated. And chagrined. And annoyed with her. And, reluctantly, impressed by her.

Miss Penrose returned then with a large cart. "The maids use this to transport linens to and fro, since they must often carry many sets," she explained.

Fortunately, the stairwell to the Valentine room was in this wing of the house. Sol called Mr. Havner inside and with his help, he rolled Allinton's limp form onto the cart and covered it with a tablecloth she had brought with her, then wheeled him to the stairwell. Thankfully, most servants were helping their masters dress for dinner or helping to prepare dinner, so they encountered no one.

Sol and Mr. Havner carried Allinton up the stairs—a laborious process that made Sol feel every ache in his joints as he huffed and puffed—and then into the Valentine room. While Sol sucked breath into his lungs, Laura's twin eleven-year-old servants appeared as if from thin air and helped Mr. Havner tie Allinton to a wooden chair using some complicated knot Sol had never seen before.

"Is this ..." Laura's eyes circled the room, and while she didn't comment on it, Sol could see she wanted to laugh. "... an appropriate place to speak to him?"

"Yes. It's where I was when your note reached me."

Sol looked at the servants uncomfortably. While they'd helped him, and knew more about this than he wanted, he didn't want to speak to Allinton in front of them. But Laura seemed to understand that, because she nodded to them and they left the room.

Laura, however, stayed and gave Sol a narrow gaze that seemed to challenge him to try to oust her from the upcoming conversation. She probably deserved to remain, considering what she had already uncovered on her own.

Wordlessly, she offered Sol her vial of hartshorn to wake Allinton. What was she, of the iron constitution and even more implacable will, doing with hartshorn? He lifted an eyebrow at her.

"I bring it when I'm with my mother," she explained. "She likes to get 'episodes' when I'm doing something she doesn't like."

Ah, that sounded like Mrs. Cambrook.

Sol opened the odorous vial and placed it under Allinton's nose, and after a moment, he jerked violently. His eyes were bleary and half-opened, but they squinted perhaps in pain as they roved around the violently pink room.

"Now then—"

"Wait, Sol." Laura turned to Miss Penrose. "What is your name, dear?"

"You may call me Mary, my lady."

"Mary, I realize you are not a true maid, but as you are dressed for the part, would you be so kind as to fetch us some tea?"

"This is not a tea party," Sol barked at her.

She faced him with the sharp bronze of her eyes. "Have you been knocked unconscious before? I have. Mr. Allinton will be more likely to speak coherently, especially after being hit on the head, if he has some sugar and liquids in him."

The mention of being knocked unconscious was a dash of ice water on his irritation. Yes, she would know how Allinton would be feeling right about now.

Also if it were any other prisoner, this would be ludicrous, but since this was Allinton, Sol saw the wisdom in her words and grunted. He noticed that Miss Penrose winked at Laura as she left the room.

"You may speak to Mr. Allinton all you wish after he has had a little tea," Laura said, "but until then, may I clean his cut?"

The blow to the back of his head hadn't bled much, but there were a few drops on the collar of his jacket.

Out of sight of Allinton, Sol gave her a fierce, questioning glare, *What are you doing?* which she returned with an equally fierce admonition, *Just trust me.*

Trust her? This was *his* mission into which she'd inserted herself. And yet, Laura hardly never did or said anything without some deeper motivation. She might deliberately sound empty-headed when it suited her, but she always had some goal behind it.

So, he sighed and made a grand gesture of, *By all means, after you.*

Laura took out her handkerchief, bent down behind Allinton, and began dabbing at the large lump at the back of his head. She began talking to him in a low voice. "I'm sure this is very confusing for you, so I'll explain. Sol is the one who knocked you out, but he and my coachman carried you to this room, which Sol says is safe from prying eyes and ears. And while his method of securing this audience with you is quite violent, I really do believe he doesn't wish to clap you in chains. Otherwise he'd have bundled you up in a coach and you'd be halfway to London by now."

"Your voice ..." Allinton mumbled.

"I beg your pardon?"

"Your voice is spellbinding," he said slowly. "It kept me from escaping."

She paused, then said, "I'm not surprised."

"What?" Sol asked involuntarily.

"Why?" Allinton asked.

"The entire time I was talking to you in the library, I was praying for you not to move until Sol finally arrived. God must have answered my prayer."

Allinton snorted. "Of course He would. He'd have no care for a thief." The self-loathing saturated his voice.

"God was crucified with two thieves," Laura said gently. "One criminal mocked him, but the other asked forgiveness and Jesus rewarded him with paradise. Which thief will you be?"

In a scoffing voice, he replied, "Are you saying you're God?"

Sol responded without thinking. "I'm saying this as your mentor. I can't believe you'd do this without a reason. I wanted to talk to you rather than simply bringing you in."

Sol was standing on Allinton's side with only a view of his profile, but he clearly saw the pained anguish in his expression. He wanted to believe Sol ... but couldn't, for some reason.

That reason drifted into his head like dark wispy shadows. And suddenly he knew he had to convince Allinton to trust in him. It was more important than the younger man could possibly guess.

But before acting, he glanced at Laura. She felt his gaze and turned to him.

She shouldn't know these things he was doing. She shouldn't have seen Miss Penrose, shouldn't have learned she was helping Sol. But what could he do? He couldn't make her unsee these things.

However, she was remarkably calm about all of this, which made him suspect that she had already guessed that he was doing something secretive for the government, although he didn't know how she could have found it out. But it wasn't completely surprising to him, because she was smart and observant. In fact, he had noticed just from small things she often said that her observation skills and attention to little details were on par with any agent he'd known.

He didn't want to involve her, and yet he had to take part of the blame for this. He had already involved her when he used her to get the last-minute invitation to the party. She might not have noticed his strange behavior if he'd found some other means to attend.

She had a reputation for being unconventional in certain situations, but he had never seen her use her intelligence and skills in this way. She had been blanketed by an intangible emotional fog when her husband had been alive, that made her drift through society as only a vague presence. Since his death, she'd become a clearer presence with a reputation as a woman who helped those in need.

She was probably infuriated at him for using her in order to gain entrance to the party, and yet she had helped him. She was also kind to Allinton, just as Sol still believed he was a good man.

He couldn't refuse her help, although he wanted to. But she would be offended if he tried to push her out now, and it wasn't her fault that he was feeling so impotent and angry at himself, that he was unsure of his course because he didn't know how to handle a situation where he'd received help from an outside source.

But he couldn't afford to be unsure. He had to lead his team, who were looking to him for direction.

And so he made a decision that may anger his superiors, but he would pay the price. If he were going to force her to leave, he should have done it earlier. He had to trust her silence.

At that moment, Miss Penrose returned, and she had brought Mr. Neybridge with her. He had been following Allinton this afternoon on his visit to Mrs. Fairbanks's relation, but Sol guessed that he had been outstripped by the carriage back to Helsey Park. Otherwise, he would have seen Allinton enter the library or arrived to help Sol to capture him.

He was unsurprised by Laura's presence, so Miss Penrose

must have told him what happened. His eyebrows rose as Laura gave Allinton some tea, but otherwise he said nothing.

Sol grabbed another wooden chair—this one thin and spindly —to set directly in front of Allinton, and he worried he might break it as he sat gingerly. "Allinton, look at me."

The man slowly raised his face.

In a gentle voice, he said, "I trained you for a year. We went on missions together. Please tell me why you are doing this. If you are in some sort of financial straits or some type of danger ..."

The words seemed to be ripped from Allinton's parted lips. "It isn't me, Drydale. It's my family."

He had guessed as much. This man had been willing to face down death a handful of times, and he would not steal from innocent people for mere coin or a personal threat. "What about them?"

"If I don't obey them, my family will be killed." There were dark shadows behind his eyes. "They told me exactly what to steal. I didn't want to ... we tried to escape them, but couldn't."

"Who threatened you?"

But Allinton shook his head and looked miserable.

The dark suspicions in Sol's mind solidified into the thing he had been dreading. If someone had given Allinton instructions about stealing specific items in secure safe boxes, it meant that they knew exactly what he could do, they knew his specialty.

And only *someone from the Ramparts* would know that.

Neybridge and Miss Penrose realized the truth just as Sol did, and while the older gentleman simply looked a little more grim, the young woman grew slightly pale.

This was why Allinton was reluctant to trust him. But how could Sol convince him he wasn't the one to betray him?

"Think, Stewart. If I were the one who told them about you, I'd want you to sell those gemstones and the folio. I wouldn't have gone through all this trouble to stop you. But you must have guessed I found the gems in your pockets, and the folio is not leaving this house. You were going to deliver them to the buyer tonight, weren't you? That's why you chose this time and not some point in the middle of the night to steal it."

Allinton searched Sol's face, trying to decide if Sol were telling the truth.

"If you tell me everything, Stewart, I swear to you that I will help you and your family escape. I swear it on my life."

His vehement words had shocked Allinton. Hesitantly, he said, "When I was first contacted, I didn't tell anyone at the department because ... they don't usually care about our families."

"I am not speaking as the department. I am speaking as your friend. I have changed much in the past several years." He glanced at Laura, realizing she was the reason. "I don't blame you for not trusting our superiors, but I am begging you to trust me."

Allinton broke Sol's gaze, hanging his head and staring at the ground. The silence was thick between them, and yet when Sol happened to look up at Laura, she was smiling slightly.

Finally Allinton said, "I am to deliver the gems and folio to a buyer who will meet me at the old abbey ruins on the estate grounds tonight."

Sol slowly released the breath he'd been holding. "Why is he meeting you here?"

"He wanted the folio as soon as possible before it was discovered to be missing, for Lord Meynhill will surely search the house and the guests' rooms."

"Do you know the buyer?"

"I met him once. Fergus Gordon."

Sol shook his head. "I don't know him."

"I recognize his name," Laura said. "Lady Marchell wrote down a list of all the collectors she knew who would be interested in those gems and the folio, and his name was on it."

"And after the trade?" Sol asked.

"I received a note to deliver the item to a delivery location in London by tomorrow morning."

"They wanted you to travel all night to London?"

Allinton gave a one-shoulder shrug. "When they saw that I could easily gain access to the homes of the gemstone owners, they began demanding more and more of me, warning of harm to my family if I didn't obey."

"Did they do anything?"

Allinton's mouth grew grim. "When they first left me a message with instructions and threatening my family, I refused. But then the next day, a stranger attacked my wife and son on their way home from the village. Both of them were injured, but not badly."

Laura put a hand to her mouth, but otherwise remained calm. Miss Penrose's eyes flashed, and her jaw grew tight. Mr. Neybridge noticed and placed a calming hand on her arm, which made her relax again.

Allinton continued, "So we attempted to leave. We had booked passage on a ship bound for the colonies, but some of their men found us at the docks."

"Stewart," Sol said, "if I'd known ..."

"You'd have told your superiors, and they would have instructed me to let my wife act as bait to draw them out," Allinton snapped.

Sol opened his mouth to retort, but then closed it again. Sir Derrick might not have wanted to do that, but others in the department would. They'd have pressured Sir Derrick to order Allinton to put his family in danger, and who would he have tasked with keeping Mrs. Allinton safe? Fewer agents than normal, because he wouldn't know who to trust since one of them betrayed Allinton.

Laura suddenly stepped close and laid a soft hand on the ex-agent's arm, which was still tied to the arms of the chair. "I know you only desire to keep them safe, but what will happen once you have delivered the item to them?"

She hadn't said it, but the implication was clear, and they all knew what wasn't being said. Allinton and his family would likely be killed after he had done what they wanted him to do.

Sol said, "The only way for you to be safe is to capture Mr. Gordon. We can find out what he knows about who arranged this deal, and if he is not the one who betrayed you, we can uncover his identity from there. Is Gordon the one who is telling you what to do?"

Allinton shook his head. "I believe it is someone different. The one time I met Gordon, he mentioned the written instructions I received as though they came from someone else, not himself. And the notes referred to Gordon as a different person from the author."

"You have never met the person sending the notes?"

"No."

"Where is the last note you received?"

Allinton hesitated, then sighed. "The false heel of my boot."

Sol's knees hurt as he knelt to tug off Allinton's Hessians. He still ached from his tumble on top of Georgina Edson earlier today. It was depressing to admit that he was getting old.

Inside the boot, underneath a thick flap that covered the heel, the space was hollow. A folded paper had been stuffed inside.

The handwriting was not familiar to him, but it was sharp and masculine, with bold strokes.

But before he read the note, his eye was arrested by a red symbol stamped on the bottom of the page.

He couldn't have expected this. After all, Allinton had been betrayed by a mole within the Ramparts, not the Foreign Office. At the very least, he should have been more in control of his reactions.

But the sight of that symbol made him gasp slightly. And someone as observant as Laura Glencowe, Lady Wynwood, most certainly noticed his reaction of surprise.

No, he didn't recognize the handwriting. But he recognized that symbol, which meant that this entire affair had nothing to do with gemstones.

It had to do with treason.

Laura had never seen Sol like this, with this commanding air. To the rest of society, he was a genial gentleman of means, affable and perhaps a bit frivolous, with a keen mind that was feared and respected by his club's chess players, but unwilling to exert himself to use it for anything other than games.

But this man before her, who built a complex plan from the scraps of information he'd just been given, was a stranger to her.

And yet not a stranger. She had seen glimpses of it throughout the years, although he hid it well. It was why she had suspected he had been involved in something more secretive and important with the government. She happened to be by his side when he spoke to certain men, and she noticed a strange firmness in his voice, words unsaid under the jovial meaningless conversation between himself and an acquaintance. And because this Stranger-Sol peeked out only when he spoke with men known to work in the Home Office, she had drawn her own conclusions. She hadn't needed to know the full story, and so she hadn't asked or investigated it.

But now this Stranger-Sol was standing in front of her. She knew he was not best pleased with her and dissatisfied with himself, concerned for Allinton and fearful of something that involved the author of those letters. But he shoved all that aside to be Stranger-Sol now, a commanding officer and not a society gentleman.

And yet this commanding officer had allowed her to stay and be a part of this. He'd had the right to force her to leave before he began speaking to Allinton. She would have been unhappy, perhaps even furious at him, but she would have done as he asked of her.

She had seen the respect in his eyes, and it warmed her. There were many things he did that caused a warmth in her chest or a tightening in her belly. Things she ignored because although it had been ten years, she wasn't certain she was ready to trust a man again, even if the man were Sol.

No, this Stranger-Sol did not alarm her because she had seen shades of him through the years of her friendship with him. What alarmed her were the roles of the people in this dangerous play.

She had never known a woman like Mary (which was obviously not her name). There was an underlying elegance and refinement to her diction and her movements that hinted she had been raised in a wealthy and high-born house, but it had been almost erased by the hollow darkness in her eyes. There was also something about her face that reminded Laura of someone, but she couldn't recall who.

And yet this young woman, who might have been a noblewoman in other circumstances, was given a major role in this play, without regard for her gender or her slender form.

Mr. Allinton had been released from his restraints, although no one could figure out how to untie the knots the twins had made, so Sol had cut him free. He now sat drinking tea and wolfing down the biscuits Mary had brought, discussing some difficult points of the plan.

Mary was planning to leave to prepare, so Laura asked her, "Shall I help you, dear? I can dress the wig."

The young woman hesitated, glancing at where Sol, Allinton, and the other man—"David"—were in a discussion. "It would be helpful," she admitted. "It's a frightful mess since I simply stuffed it into my satchel."

"I am not as skilled as my maid, but I doubt Sol would wish

to involve anyone else. I tried to convince him my servants were most capable."

Mary smiled slightly, a gentle curve of her mouth with a shadow of sadness to it. "He worries about anyone else becoming injured. And while Mr. Havner is very strong, he is unlikely to have much experience in a certain branch of fighting in which we have been trained."

Laura would have asked more about it, but she knew the woman wouldn't tell her.

She followed Mary all the way to the carriage house. There weren't any grooms or stable boys about at this hour—they were likely tending to the horses in the adjoining stables—and so the darkened space echoed hollowly as they both climbed inside a plain carriage not unlike the ones used by the servants of the other houseguests. Mary lit one of the carriage lamps so that they could see, and she retrieved a satchel from the corner, withdrawing a smaller bag that contained a blonde wig.

It had once been a grand wig from the time of Laura's mother's societal debut, but the locks had been brushed free of powder and had once been tucked into a plain chignon, which was now in disarray.

"Do you often travel with a wig?"

Mary hesitated, then decided to answer her. "I always bring a light-colored wig with me, in the event I need a disguise." As she gathered her brown hair, Laura noticed that it had fine glints of gold in it. It reminded her of one of her cousins, who had been blonde in her youth but had grown into a brunette in her teen years. When Mary tucked the hair under a fine silk stocking cap, Laura also noticed a thin scar just under her left jaw, barely noticeable.

She positioned the wig firmly atop her head and Laura was struck by how much it changed her. She had a fine-boned but slightly androgynous face, and the specter of pain in her dark eyes contributed to her more masculine air.

They sat in the dim carriage and Mary positioned herself so that the light from the carriage lamp would shine upon her. Laura sat next to her and began undoing the chignon, sticking the pins through the fabric of the cloak she'd donned when she had planned to surprise Mr. Allinton from the double library doors leading to the garden.

"I will not ask you not to do this," Laura said slowly. "We hardly know each other. And yet I cannot help but be alarmed to see a young woman put herself into danger. Are you accustomed to this?"

"One never gets accustomed to this." An unpleasant memory gave a slight edge to her voice.

"Have you done this often?"

"I cannot tell you that, my lady."

"Of course. Forgive me." She brushed out the brittle locks of hair.

There were many minutes of silence, but then Mary said quietly, "Although I would not normally have chosen a life doing these things ... now that I have been put upon this path, in a strange way, I believe it fits me."

Laura was shocked. "A life of secrets and danger fits you?"

"Rather, it fits the person I have become. The circumstances in my life ... made me into someone who fits this life."

Laura could not imagine the kinds of circumstances that would do that, but she did know anguish when she heard it. And guilt. "Yes," she said slowly. "Circumstances can shape us into people we would never have expected to be."

"I appreciate your concern, my lady," Mary said quickly. "I have only had two people in my life who would care."

Only two? Laura's heart began to ache for this young woman.

She continued, "But I chose this lifestyle freely. In some ways, I think the Lord created me to do this. And they ... I have been trained to handle these sorts of demands upon me."

What kinds of training had she gone through? The same as

Sol and Mr. Allinton? And yet Laura recalled the fondness in the eyes of the other older man, David, and the fact that Mary and David worked smoothly together, a team long-used to each other's ways. Perhaps he was one of those "two" she had mentioned.

"All the training in the world cannot always protect you." Laura was sticking pins into the reformed chignon rather haphazardly. Aya would have screamed in horror. "You are putting yourself at risk, just like any man. But no one is invincible."

"But I choose to do this." Mary turned to look at Laura, causing her to lose her grip on the loose, drooping bun. "I choose to put myself at risk to protect others. Wouldn't you do the same?" The charcoal-colored eyes studied her, and Laura felt laid bare.

"Yes, I would." She had not always been that type of person, but the Lady Wynwood she was now would do it in a heartbeat.

"I should be asking if you are so sanguine about your role," Mary said. "It is not without risks."

Sol had not been sanguine about involving Laura, but it became clear while they were talking that he had originally brought Mary and David with the intention of only bringing in Mr. Allinton. Now that Mary and David had their own separate role in this dangerous farce, even with Mr. Allinton's willing help, he was in need of other actors.

Laura had been hesitant, but had volunteered to help him. Sol had immediately refused. However, it had not been difficult to convince him eventually.

"I'll hardly be in danger since my role is so small." Laura kept her voice light, although she knew she was not allaying the young woman's fears for her. "In contrast, you will be putting yourself directly in harm's way."

"I will not lie and say I will not be in a dangerous position," Mary said as she turned back around, "but I fully understand

what I might need to do. I have accepted it, and I am prepared
for it."

Laura reformed the bun, with better results this time. She
was deeply impacted by this woman's courage as she faced
danger. She was certain men had to face great physical peril
with courage on the battlefield, but she had never thought
about women who would choose to do so.

Lord, I still worry about her.

But even as she prayed it, she realized that she needed to let
this go and trust her Heavenly Father to be watching out for
Mary. The woman was not her daughter or even her family, and
she had made these choices on her own. And who better than
God to keep His eyes upon her, and hold His hands under her
to catch her if she should fall?

And yet there was something powerful Laura could do for
her.

As she stuck in the last pin, she asked, "May I pray for you?"

Mary turned, and there was surprise, but also warmth in her
gaze, and some of the dark ghosts that always lingered there
were shoved back for a short time. "Of course."

And so she grasped the woman's hands and prayed, with
words that were drawn from her heart and weighted down with
her respect and concern for Mary, but given up to God with the
trust that He was watching and listening.

Chapter Seven

Allinton had walked into danger countless times before. But this time, his family's life was at stake, and he was forced to trust others to protect them.

It made him grind his teeth, and a knot in his stomach kept growing tighter and tighter as he rode his horse over the uneven grass up the slope.

The ancient abbey was little more than a few large stones piled here and there, with a single fragment of a wall that reached barely seven feet high, so calling it a "ruin" was a bit of an exaggeration. But in the looming darkness of twilight, the stones were like trolls huddled at the top of the small hill where the abbey had once stood.

Allinton was nearly at the top before two shadows peeled themselves away from a stone and came toward him.

Neither of them was Gordon. The man in front was nearly as tall as he was wide, and his rather small round head had pale hair cut very short, so that he almost appeared bald. Even in the dim light, Allinton could make out flat dark eyes and a bulbous nose over a mouth pulled tight in an almost-sneer.

Behind the huge hulking figure stood another man, not nearly so wide but almost as tall. He carried himself with a loose, fluid grace that made it seem he was always in motion, a slow, catlike movement even when he was standing still. His face was pale and dominated by a very badly broken nose, but otherwise plain and unassuming. His hair was also the same shade as the other man's, and similarly cut very short.

"You're late," the giant man grunted.

"Gordon's the one who wanted to meet after dark in an unfamiliar area. I didn't want to push my horse in the dark or it might have been injured. And then I got lost."

He dismounted stiffly. He still felt the pain from Drydale's blow to his skull. The man might be older than he was, but he had heavier hands, and despite all their training, he'd never been on the receiving end of a blow like that before.

He shouldn't be trusting him. But from the moment he first spotted him in the crowd at the Venetian breakfast, he had *wanted* to trust him. But his fear kept him moving forward on the wretched path he'd been set on.

The giant man roughly searched through his pockets and even his hat to make sure he wasn't hiding anything. He peeked into the satchel Allinton carried but all he would see were the three bulging cloth bags and the pasteboard box.

At last he pointed Allinton up the slope to the shadow of the broken wall, and Mr. Gordon stepped out as he drew near.

He was a short man, and slim, with neat brown hair and slightly bulging eyes. His front tooth stuck out slightly between his lips, making it look as though he were constantly sucking on a sweet.

"Let's get this over with, Gordon." Allinton held out the satchel, but the buyer held up an imperious hand.

"We wait before we do business." His high-pitched voice carried over the night breezes that swirled among the rocks.

"Wait? For what?"

"You were late, which makes me suspicious." The bulging eyes narrowed.

"As I told your man, I got lost."

"We'll see."

"That's rich, for you to tell me to wait after complaining I was late. Do you want to do business or not?"

The man's mouth screwed up into a jagged line. "I won't open the trade until my man comes back to ensure all is well!" he snapped.

His man? Meaning, a third man besides the two behind him?

Allinton fought to hide his shiver, which wasn't from the wind.

When he'd met Gordon before, it had been directly after the first theft. The letter writer had instructed him to meet because Gordon was insisting on inspecting the stolen sapphire, but Allinton wasn't to allow him to keep the gemstone.

Gordon had had two men with him, the two who had met him earlier and searched his pockets. Allinton had assumed he would only bring the two, since "Tiny" and "Nose" were enough.

But apparently Gordon had brought three.

Allinton knew he could beat Tiny. He'd watched the man move and knew he favored his left shoulder and right knee, and he'd occasionally rub his right hip in an unobtrusive way. The other man, Nose, moved with quick actions, but not in a way that implied he'd been trained in fighting.

Allinton knew nothing about the third man. And he also knew he and Drydale couldn't take on all three and win.

It was also a professional disgrace that he hadn't noticed he was being followed when he had saddled his horse and rode from the stables. Thank God he'd actually circled a bit as if lost before heading toward the abbey ruins.

Would God watch over tonight, as Lady Wynwood seemed to think? For him, religion was only on the outskirts of his life and his thoughts, but the dire position in which his family had been placed suddenly made him want to cling to her faith like a drowning man. And he somehow knew that God would listen to her prayers.

Would He listen to Stewart's prayers too?

God, please help us.

He received no answer, no sudden feeling of power or presence. And yet there was a part of his mind that seemed to tell him that he was not alone.

Allinton stared hard at Gordon as he waited, and the small man smirked at him. "I can tell you don't like the way I do things."

Allinton didn't answer him and looked away.

"But I also know that you can't do anything about it." He gave a snide laugh.

He kept his gaze averted from Gordon, even though what he really wanted to do was punch the man's lights out.

Gordon chortled, "In fact, you will do everything my client tells you to do."

"If that's the case, then why bother to check that I'm truly alone?" he couldn't resist snapping at him.

Gordon just laughed again, although the wind took it away. They stood there for long minutes as it grew darker and colder.

Finally Gordon broke the silence. "By the way, I commend you on those safe boxes. Truly marvelous work."

Once, Allinton had been proud of his ability, because he knew that he was exercising it for the good of his country. When stealing the gemstones, he'd only wanted to vomit.

"I'd heard you were good, but I had no idea you'd be so bold. During three parties, no less."

It had been the note-writer who ordered such urgency, who had demanded he get it done during those parties. He'd been forced to find a way to attend events he hadn't been invited to, and then to slip away and break into safes he hadn't investigated or researched ahead of time.

But since Gordon was in so chatty a mood, he might as well take advantage of it. "How did you even know about me?"

Gordon gave a sly smile. "A mutual friend."

If someone from the Ramparts told him about Allinton, had he also told him about the Ramparts? This mysterious "mutual friend" had known not only about Allinton's specialty, but also about his family and how to most effectively apply pressure on him to do their bidding.

He wondered if Gordon was telling him these things because he believed Allinton was unlikely to survive long after delivering the package.

He heard soft footsteps only a moment before a third man appeared from behind the broken wall. Allinton hadn't even heard his approach, the man was that skilled at hiding his presence. It was too dark to see him clearly beyond a shadowy figure in the gloom.

Gordon glanced at the third man, who grunted to him.

"Good." Gordon then bent at his feet and Allinton realized there was a lantern there. Then his eyesight was blinded by the spark from a flint and the flare from the lit lantern.

At the same time, the satchel was tugged from his hand and Tiny handed it to Gordon. The small man's eyes gleamed as he reached inside and pulled out a cloth pouch with a hard round object the size of a small chicken's egg. But upon feeling it, he suddenly frowned.

He ripped open the bag and shook the stone into his hand. His mouth pulled wide into a feral snarl.

"What are you doing?" He opened the other sacks and shook out the other stones—smooth rocks pilfered from among those that lined the walkways of Lord Meynhill's garden. The pasteboard box was savagely torn open to reveal the newspaper tucked inside.

Gordon hadn't even signaled before Tiny's giant hand wrapped around Allinton's neck. The pressure made his head feel like it was going to explode off his shoulders, while the pain traveled all the way up his jaw to his cheekbones. He gasped silently.

"What's the meaning of this?" Gordon demanded.

Allinton gave his best imitation of a goldfish.

Gordon sighed and signaled to Tiny, who released him. He bent at the waist and inhaled sharply, but that only made his neck hurt even more. He panted in shallow breaths as the stars faded from in front of his eyes.

"Answer me!" Gordon said.

Allinton deliberately took a few more breaths before he did, just to annoy the small man. "I'll lead you to the real gems and the folio if you'll sweeten the deal for me."

Gordon stared at him for a heartbeat, then suddenly burst into laughter. But it was a razor-edged sound that held no mirth. "You would really dare to do this? You have no leverage here. You're here only to obey."

"If that's true, then why are you holding three stones and a newspaper?"

Gordon crumpled the paper, which he hadn't realized he was still holding, and dashed it to the ground. "You're a fool."

"You're wasting time. The folio and gems are in the house. As soon as they discover the folio is missing, they'll search the house and find everything, and then put them all under stronger security. Even I won't be able to get them after that."

"Do you think you're so special that you can't be replaced?"

"If I wasn't, you'd have found someone else to do the job willingly for you."

Gordon's face contorted into an ugly mask, snarling lips and arching eyebrows, eyes gleaming with rage in the light from the lantern.

"Tick-tock." Allinton's throat still hurt but it no longer pained him to breathe. Gordon needed to act soon. He had to secure the items before Lord Meynhill noticed his precious folio was stolen.

"What do you want?"

"Not much. I knew you wouldn't carry too much cash. A

thousand pounds."

"I don't carry that much."

"Of course you do. You strike me as a man who likes to be prepared for any contingency. Of course you'd have cash squirreled away in your luggage, in your pockets, and in other unexpected places."

Gordon's nostrils flared as he glared at Allinton. "Two hundred."

"Six."

"Fine."

He agreed so readily because Allinton had guessed he carried twice or even three times that much with him, and he was likely unwilling to waste time haggling.

"You think you're so clever, trying to swindle me?"

"Don't be upset. You're not the only one I'll be swindling."

Another sharp bark of laughter. "You're going to pull the same thing on *them*?"

"And why not? They've caused me enough grief. But now I'm finally holding something they want."

"You ..." Gordon called him something incredibly colorful that Allinton hadn't heard before even from the residents of the dingiest parts of the major cities of Europe.

"You seem terribly upset," Allinton observed.

"Because *they'll* find some way to blame me for all of this! And you'll get us *both* on their list of men they most want to hunt down."

He was likely right ... if Allinton was truly intending to try to turn on the letter writer. He noted that Gordon had referred several times to *them.* Not a single man, but more than one. Two? Or a group?

Gordon looked at Allinton with pure hatred. "I should just kill you now."

Allinton heard Tiny's knuckles crack as he made a fist. "I know why you want those gemstones and folio. They're irreplaceable. If you kill me, you won't get a thing."

"If I kill you, I won't lose anything, either. Including my head."

Gordon was still undecided. Allinton's life hinged upon this moment, and yet strangely he felt no fear. Perhaps Lady Wynwood's prayers were working. Perhaps his own were.

"Fine," Gordon said as if spitting out a bug he'd accidentally swallowed. "Fine, fine. Where are we going?"

"I'll take you there."

Drydale had warned him that this would require all his acting skills, all the finer points of manipulation that he'd learned. But he had known he would do anything if it would keep his family safe.

He wanted to feel relief, but it was still only halfway into the battle.

He walked to his horse, then followed as Gordon headed down the slope, his lantern barely lighting the few feet ahead.

"I think you're being very foolish to try to trick those people," Gordon ranted.

So it was more than two people behind this. And Gordon obviously feared them a great deal.

"Even I know not to double-cross them," Gordon added.

Allinton didn't answer. No matter how dangerous, Drydale would have to deal with them, if he kept his promise to help Stewart and his family to escape to safety.

At the bottom of the slope they retrieved their horses. Tiny's poor mount looked like it might collapse under the big man's weight.

Four of them. And only himself and Drydale to subdue them.

And Lady Wynwood, he reminded himself.

But what could a gentlewoman do? She certainly couldn't fight one of them.

Hadn't she mentioned something about her coachman earlier? Drydale had expressly forbidden any more civilians from becoming involved, but surely Lady Wynwood would keep a man about her for protection. Perhaps he would be inclined to lend a hand.

They rode back toward the manor house, going at a faster clip once they reached the well-maintained roadway. Allinton strove to appear unconcerned, but within, his worry slowly grew.

There was no way to warn Drydale. This wasn't looking good.

But there was nothing he could do.

It was already not an ideal situation, and it had just gotten worse.

Sol had swung himself up onto the rafters of the small, old boathouse on the edge of the man-made lake on the manor house grounds. There was a slight gap between the roof and the back wall of the boathouse, and Sol could see Helsey Park up the slope, ablaze with lights.

Sol could also see five horsemen approaching the boathouse. That was one more than they had bargained for.

Sol counted again, just to be sure he hadn't mistaken it in the darkness. Yes, Mr. Gordon had brought three men with him, not two.

Sol groaned and rested his forehead against the molding wood of the rafters. Wonderful, just wonderful.

As an agent out in the field, he had encountered bad odds before, and they had always managed by the skin of their teeth. This wasn't any different, surely?

Except that he was fifteen years older than he'd been, and his team consisted of only one other man, plus a noblewoman. These odds were quite possibly the worst he'd ever encountered.

He was glad, now, that he'd made sure that Laura had her coachman with her, wherever she was hiding out in that darkness. But Mr. Havner had admitted he had been in very few fights in his life, despite his large frame and above-average strength. What could he do if Gordon's men were experienced fighters?

Sol tried to tell himself that was unlikely. After all, he'd fought few men trained as well as the men of the Ramparts.

Except that Gordon had most certainly hired them as bodyguards. So they weren't there for their pretty looks.

Allinton led them directly to the boathouse. Even from his vantage point and in the darkness, Sol could tell that Gordon was wary of the enclosed space.

"Weeks." Gordon jerked his chin at the boathouse.

The giant man had already dismounted from his horse, and he now lumbered toward the open door with a lantern. Sol held his breath as he entered the small space, searching with the lantern held high, passing almost directly beneath him.

After a few moments that seemed like years, Weeks went to the door and grunted to Gordon to indicate the building was empty.

"Yates, stay out here." Gordon spoke to the shortest of his bodyguards, then gestured toward the door as he said to Allinton, "After you."

Sol could tell Allinton was tense from his posture, but then he lost sight of them as they went round to the door.

Despite his nervousness, Allinton strode confidently into the building, his booted steps ringing in counterpoint to the lapping of the water on the open end of the building. "It's over here." He gestured to the far end of the room.

"Wait." Gordon had paused by the door, looking at something on the outside of the creaking piece of wood. He gestured and said, "Weeks, take care of that."

Then the giant man left the building and swung around to the outside of the door. Sol heard him grunt, and the door jerked a few times. Then the sound of wood splintering, and he might have also heard a soft thud of metal dropping to the ground. Weeks had broken the bolt that locked the door from the outside.

He had destroyed the one part that their entire ambush hinged upon. The odds had gone from bad to dreadful.

The men passed below Sol—first Allinton, then the seller, trailed by two of his men. Sol hesitated, but decided that since Allinton knew these men, he'd surely signal Sol with what he wanted to do.

Weeks remained by the door, but Allinton drew him away by saying, "Tiny, help me move this, will you?"

Weeks scowled at Allinton, but left his post to step closer to him. "Help with what?" His voice was thick and low.

Allinton delivered a swift, sharp kick at Week's right knee.

That was the signal, then.

Sol dropped down from the rafters. He was in between Gordon and his guard, but he opted to attack Gordon first and knock him to the ground. The man's head hit the floorboards with a hard *thump*, and he lay there, dazed.

Sol took advantage to kick out at the guard.

The one thing they must do was ensure Gordon did not escape. Originally Laura was to sneak up on the boathouse and lock the door from the outside. The building was still open at one end to the lake, but Mr. Havner had said he could at least hold Gordon if he escaped in that direction while Sol and Allinton dealt with the more experienced fighters, Gordon's guards.

Except the door lock was now broken, and there was a third guard outside who would come in any moment now.

Except … he never did.

Sol swung punches and shot jabs at the guard, trying to find an opening to knock the man unconscious. He only caught glimpses of Allinton and the giant Weeks, but the agent was younger and faster than Sol, and he knew he could handle himself.

Sol caught a blow to the side of his head that made his ear ring, but he traded with a solid hit to the man's torso. The guard gave a pained *oof*, but was still quick to follow with another punch from his other hand, aimed at Sol's nose. He dodged just in time.

But then a figure ran behind the guard, and Sol realized Gordon had recovered from the blow he'd given to him. He was sprinting for the wide open doorway.

If he escaped, they had failed.

Sol redoubled his efforts, desperation fueling his attacks, but the guard had a slight smile as he understood Sol's state of mind. He positioned himself between Sol and Gordon's retreating figure.

Sol thought he saw an opening. He feinted toward the man's left side, then swung the fist into an uppercut.

Except the guard's right hand came swinging around so fast it was only a blur. Knuckles hit Sol squarely in the jaw.

His vision both darkened and turned into a multitude of stars. He couldn't move his limbs. He thought he might have been falling, but he wasn't certain until his back slammed into the floor.

He didn't land flat on his back, and his head was turned enough that he saw Gordon's feet hurrying toward the open door.

He was going to escape.

Laura carefully guided the dogcart along the narrow trail through the trees, then emerged into the clear space all around the lakefront boathouse. The man standing guard a few yards from the door to the building spotted her immediately because of the small lantern hung on the cart.

"Oh, thank goodness you're here," she said as she drew near. "I need your help."

"I can't help you," the man said rudely. "Go to the house for help." He jerked his head toward the blazing lights of the manor house, a mile or two distant across the wide lawn and up a gentle slope.

"No, I am afraid it must be you." She infused as much imperiousness into her tone as she'd ever heard from one of the patronesses of Almack's in refusing a voucher. "Kindly take my horse and cart back to the stables."

"Take it yourself." Even in the dim light from the lantern, she could see his eyes glaring at her. She might have been frightened if she hadn't known her coachman was sneaking up behind him.

And then there came a rather loud thump from within the building. And the man turned around and spotted Mr. Havner barely five feet away from him.

Well, that certainly did not go as planned.

The guard swung a fist at Mr. Havner, but his motions were slow and he blocked it easily. The coachman hit the guard in the torso, but even Laura could tell his motions were unpracticed. The guard barely flinched at the blow.

But then two dark shadows came whistling toward them and hit the guard in the back. He would have cried out in pain but Mr. Havner had shoved his hand under the man's chin, forcing his head back, and the guard could only give a muffled groan. They twisted, and the lantern glinted off of two tiny throwing knives buried in the meaty part of his shoulders, courtesy of her eleven-year-old twins. Their accuracy with knives was second to none, although they never spoke of how they had used their skills on the streets.

Mr. Havner had managed to move behind the man, and his meaty forearm now cradled the guard's neck. The man slapped at Mr. Havner's head and shoulders, then scrabbled at his forearm, but he couldn't break his grip.

Laura had no time to waste. "Jump out," she ordered the twins in the dogcart, then slapped the reins and rushed toward the closed boathouse door.

They'd seen when the giant man had broken the lock, and she could have predicted Sol's dismay, for he must have seen it from his hiding place inside the building. But Laura had known immediately what she could to in lieu of their original plan for her to lock the door.

She drove the cart as close to the door as she could, scraping the wheels against the walls with piercing sounds.

She was none too soon. The door suddenly banged against the cart's sturdy wheels, attempting to open from the inside. It rattled again in frustration as whoever was on the other side railed against the blocked door.

Laura heaved a sigh. She'd been just in time. Next, she had to trust in Sol and Mr. Allinton.

Gordon threw himself against the door to try to open it, but it wouldn't budge. There was something outside blocking it.

Laura. Sol should have known she'd figure something out.

He kicked at the exposed knee of the man he was fighting, but he jumped out of the way enough that his foot only grazed him. However, Sol followed with an almost instantaneous kick with his other foot that connected sharply with the man's shinbone, and he cried out, stumbling.

Sol swung to his feet just in time to block the man's downward blow, then jabbed at the exposed ribs.

The sound of splashing made him glance to see Gordon moving laboriously through the water toward the open end of the boathouse. "Allinton!" he roared.

"A little busy!" came the irritated reply, but only a moment later, a loud thud made the floorboards tremble. Then more water splashing as Allinton raced after Gordon.

"He took out Weeks?" The guard shoved Sol away to gain some distance, and he saw the still form of the giant man on the ground.

They circled. He knew Sol was in a hurry, and so he made no moves toward him, just biding his time.

Fine.

Sol waited until just the right moment, then threw a roundhouse punch that swished through air. But it was only a feint to hide the kick he sent solidly into the man's stomach.

Caught off guard, he stumbled backward ... and flipped over Weeks's huge bulk.

The back of his head hit the floor with a sharp sound, and then he slumped where he lay, his legs propped up on Weeks's body.

Sol was about to follow Allinton and Gordon into the water, but then the door opened and revealed one of Laura's twins. Whatever she'd used to block the door was now gone.

As Sol raced out of the building, there was a loud *crack* that seemed to split the night. He jerked in surprise.

But it was not a pistol. It was a whip.

The lake only gradually grew deeper, so Gordon was a few yards from shore but still standing with the water only up to his waist. Mr. Havner had waded out into the water also, and now his whip had latched onto Gordon's arm. The small man's face was twisted in agony, and he grabbed at the braided leather wrapped around his limb.

Allinton was splashing toward him, so Gordon tried to run away, but he was caught by the whip and couldn't move deeper into the lake. He tried to run through the water, but Allinton came up behind him and caught him under the arms, rendering him immobile. He twisted from side to side, but couldn't break his grip.

He was captured. Sol released his breath, then regretted it as pain from his fight flared through his body.

With slow movements, Allinton was herding Gordon toward shore, with Mr. Havner keeping the whip taut around his forearm.

Sol looked toward the side away from the water, where Gordon had left the third guard, but he was on the ground, trussed up like a roast with more of those complicated knots the twins favored. The girl, Clara, was sitting on top of the man as if he were a bench in a garden, and he appeared to be unconscious.

A whinny drew his attention, and he saw Laura climbing down from the dogcart. The wheel looked a little worse for wear, and he realized she'd driven it to block the door.

"Well, that was quite exciting," she said as if they were in her drawing room having tea. "By the way, you owe my coachman a bottle of whiskey—the good stuff, and he says you would know what he meant. As for the twins, Clara would like a book and Calvin wants a pocket watch."

He hadn't exactly forbidden her from utilizing her servants, but he also hadn't expected to need their help quite so much. And since they'd already helped in capturing Allinton, he supposed they deserved at least that much, even though he was again in a position to be indebted to civilians.

He sighed. "Since I am cast into the role of St. Nicholas, what did you want from me?"

She gave him a smile that was sharper than a double-bladed knife. "A little more honesty next time. And, at your earliest convenience, a very *loud* discussion."

He wasn't looking forward to that.

Chapter Eight

Lena Penrose had ridden in the coach for five or six hours in the dark to reach Allinton's country home. Normally she wouldn't dream of calling upon a stranger at this time of night, but Mr. Allinton had been adamant. He wanted his family to be safe, or he wouldn't agree to help them. And for him, safety meant being out of the reach of whoever had been able to discover his secret past.

They had assumed the house was being watched somehow, so Lena's role in approaching Mrs. Allinton had been a matter of course. In the eight years she had been an agent with the Ramparts, she had discovered time and again that men will always underestimate and overlook a woman.

She was in luck, and there was a light in an upper window. According to what Mr. Allinton had told her, that would be their bedroom. He mentioned that his wife, Farah, often liked to remain awake an extra hour or two and read novels in bed.

She gathered her traveling cloak about her, picked up the large valise she'd pilfered from Mr. Drydale, and marched up the steps to the front door, pounding hard and persistently. The door was eventually opened by a scowling butler. He had not yet dressed for bed, but his collar was open as if he'd finally reached a point where he could relax for the evening.

He began to object, "Now, see here—"

"I have an urgent message for Mrs. Allinton," Lena said.

"The lady of the house has retired for the night," he said repressively. "I suggest you return in the morning."

"The message is from her husband."

The butler drew himself up to his full height, which was a few inches shorter than Lena, so the effect was lost on her. "I have served the Allinton's since they married, and I don't know you, young lady. Mr. Allinton would not send an 'urgent' message with a complete stranger who arrives in a harum-scarum fashion in the middle of the night."

Well, he had had point. "Mrs. Allinton will recognize the message is from her husband."

"Then give it to me and I shall relay it to her."

Everything inside her told her that he wouldn't give her the message, if he gave it at all, until the morning when it would be too late. "I won't give this message to anyone except Mrs. Allinton."

The butler sniffed. "That only makes you look even more suspicious."

"You are welcome to escort me to her as I give her the message."

"I am not inclined to allow a stranger into the house with my mistress and her child. I won't be fooled by a swindler with a questionable agenda, especially since you arrived with *that*." He pointed to the valise in her hand.

She couldn't blame him for his vigilance in protecting Mrs. Allinton and her child, but Lena wanted to protect them, too. She raised her voice and projected it through the open door. "I must see Mrs. Allinton! It's most urgent! Mrs. Allinton must receive this message! Her husband expressly asked me to deliver this message to her!"

The butler deduced her intention and tried to shut the door in her face, but she swung the valise into the space to stop it from closing.

"Mrs. Allinton! Mrs. Allinton! I have a message from your husband!"

Footsteps pattered down the stairs and a woman appeared on the staircase behind the butler, wrapped in a shawl with a frilly cap from which a blonde braid fell. "Burton? Whatever is happening?"

"Ma'am, this insolent person insists upon—"

"Mrs. Allinton, I have an urgent message from your husband!" Lena interrupted the man.

Mrs. Allinton grew very still as she stared at Lena, and her fingers trembled slightly as they tucked the shawl closer around her. "From Stewart?"

"Please, Mrs. Allinton. He said it was very important."

"This is obviously a melodramatic fabrication." Burton tried to shove the valise out of the doorway.

Mrs. Allinton stared at both of them for a long moment, and Lena tried to convey her sincerity as she held the woman's eyes while still standing firm against the butler's attempts to dislodge her from the open door.

Finally, in a weary voice, Mrs. Allinton said, "Burton, do stop. You'll break the door. Let the young woman inside."

Her guard dog yipped, "Mrs. Allinton, please! This person—"

"She appears to be very persistent. Let us listen to what she has to say." The mistress of the house then turned and began climbing back up the stairs to the first floor.

Burton gave Lena a look so sour it would have curdled her if she'd been milk, but he grudgingly opened the door a tiny fraction more, and she shoved her way inside.

He appeared torn about gracing her with the privilege of leading her to the drawing room, but he obviously didn't want her wandering around the house on her own, so he preceded her up the stairs. However, he kept turning to fasten a stern eye upon her.

Mrs. Allinton had not waited for Burton and had lit the

lamps in the cozy drawing room, but she still sat in dark shadow on the sofa when Lena entered.

"Ma'am, you mustn't sit in the dark." Burton moved a lamp to the table next to her. "I'll light the fire for you, shall I?"

"There's no need."

"Nonsense, it's quite cold—"

Mrs. Allinton raised a single elegant hand, not imperious but firm and yet gentle at the same time. It silenced him immediately. "I will not entertain my visitor for long."

That pleased Burton immensely. "Then, shall I fetch you some tea to warm you?"

Despite her brusque mention of Lena, she looked to her now with raised eyebrows. "Tea?"

"No, thank you."

"No tea, Burton. You may leave us now."

Burton appeared both pleased and displeased at the same time, but he bowed and left the room, although Lena noticed he left the door slightly cracked. He was almost overbearing in his protectiveness of Mrs. Allinton. Lena could almost suspect he harbored a *tendre* for her.

"Mrs. Allinton, you may call me Mary." She then set a finger to her lips.

The woman looked at her in confusion as Lena rose and marched across the room to the door to open it again, just in time to see Burton scurrying away. She checked, but the door had no lock. Sighing, she shut it firmly closed and returned to Mrs. Allinton. She then removed from her pocket the note Mr. Allinton had written and handed it to his wife.

She unfolded it and read it, and immediately grew so pale, she looked like a ghost in the dim lamplight.

Lena hesitated, then sat next to her on the sofa rather than returning to her seat across from her. She said in a very low voice, "I am here to help you escape with your husband, right now."

Mrs. Allinton simply stared at her for a long moment, then said while barely moving her lips, "The last time ..."

"They won't catch up to you at the docks this time. We'll see to that."

Her eyes darted around the room, as if seeing movement in the shadows. "They must have seen you arrive. How ...?"

"We have a plan. You can trust your husband's words." She nodded to the note. "And as he did, so you can trust me."

There was still fear in her eyes as she studied Lena. Then she bit her lip and looked down at her hands, thinking hard.

The minutes seemed to tick by slowly, but Lena waited. Ought she to say more? What else could she say to convince her? Time was running out. They had been racing against the clock as soon as Lena arrived, for she was surely observed by whoever was watching the Allintons.

Mrs. Allinton's lips and hands both trembled, and she suddenly rose to her feet and moved toward the door.

"Mrs. Allinton!" Lena tried not to raise her voice too much, but she couldn't help the flicker of alarm. Had she frightened her? Had she said something wrong?

But then Mrs. Allinton turned to her and put a finger to her lips, just as Lena had done earlier.

She wasn't running away from Lena. She knew what she was doing.

She left the room, and Lena expected an angry Burton to arrive and begin grilling her over her intentions toward his mistress, but she had apparently scared him enough to remain downstairs, and he didn't hear Mrs. Allinton leave the drawing room.

The house creaked and moaned, but there were no drafts in the room, nor did any flow in from the hallway outside the cracked open door. A snug building, small but right for a small family.

Except that Lena was taking them away from it all. She could understand the sense of being ripped from reality, the feeling as though her body had fallen off a cliff, when upheaval entered one's life. She could rail against fate, but one didn't choose when danger and conflict decided to plow furrows in what had once been normal.

Mrs. Allinton returned swiftly, having dressed in a traveling gown and hastily pinned up her hair. She also carried with her a small bundle wrapped in blankets. Her child was sleepy but just waking, no doubt from the sudden removal from his warm bed.

Lena opened the valise and removed a soft blanket and a vial of watered-down laudanum. She handed it to the woman to dose her groggy son—not much, just enough so that he would not cry when she had to leave the house and make the long journey, and give away his presence.

The child protested when they traded his cozy blue blanket for the brown woolen one that Lena had brought with her, but then settled back into sleep. They then nestled him inside the roomy valise. Mrs. Allinton had managed to tuck into the blanket some things she would need for a day trip with her son, and they placed it all in the valise around the baby.

"Hurry." Lena removed her cloak, which the indignant Burton had thankfully not tried to take from her, and placed it around Mrs. Allinton. She was shorter than Lena, but not by much. Lena also gave her the bonnet she'd been wearing over her blonde wig. In turn, she threw Mrs. Allinton's shawl around her shoulders.

They hesitated before leaving the room. The woman's trembling had not ceased the entire time, and it was making even Lena feel unease. She didn't know what to say to her to comfort her—there had been no one to comfort Lena in the most frightening times of her life, and she was not very soft and motherly in general. If Dorothea were here, she'd know exactly what to say.

Thoughts of Wilfrid's adopted daughter and Lena's friend

made her remember the kindness of Lady Wynwood, her concern for her in the dark carriage house, and the prayer she'd gifted to Lena before she left. That prayer had conveyed her worry over Lena, but also that she trusted in the Lord to protect her. That faith had grounded her emotions like a sudden shift to solid ground. Lady Wynwood's faith reminded Lena of Wilfrid's and Dorothea's faith, and how it had changed her from the girl she used to be.

Unbidden, a dark memory came creeping up like fog from the grass, but she turned her mind aside. She had worked to put those days completely behind her. Her only regret was the boy she'd had to leave behind without a word of goodbye.

Lena took Mrs. Allinton's hands and squeezed. Then she said a quick prayer. "Lord, be our refuge and strength."

"Amen," she whispered.

They opened the drawing room door, but Mrs. Allinton surprised Lena by shouting, "And never come back!" Then she drew the bonnet down lower over her face, buried her face in a handkerchief, and rushed out of the room. She even managed some short moans of weeping.

Lena was immensely impressed. The woman had been terribly afraid, but she was also very pragmatic. Then again, she had married a man who had been a spy, who was bold but strategic, calm-headed and disciplined. He might have been attracted to a woman who also shared those qualities, even if she wasn't a spy herself.

Lena heard Mrs. Allinton's footsteps rushing down the stairs and across the front entrance hall. She also heard Burton's footsteps, and she held her breath, but apparently Mrs. Allinton managed to exit the house before he reached the entrance hall and saw her. The door opened and slammed shut.

Burton's footsteps then climbed the stairs quickly, and Lena took one of the lamps and set it on the table near the doorway, where it would dazzle his eyes and shroud her in shadow. Then she moved to the darkness near the window, where she stood with her back to the doorway. She bundled the blue blanket into an approximation of a child and rocked it back and forth in her arms.

A tap at the door, and then Burton entered. "Ma'am, are you well? Shall I bring you the tea? Oh, the fire, you will probably be chilled—"

Lena had planned many things she could do at this moment, but in watching Mrs. Allinton, she had found a more effective tactic. She raised her hand in the same elegant, firm, gentle motion, and Burton stopped talking. She affected a sob muffled in the edge of the blanket, then made a sharp shooing motion with her hand.

"Ma'am …"

She repeated the shooing motion again, and this time Burton sighed. "As you wish, ma'am." He withdrew and closed the door behind him.

The lamp cast her figure in shadow, but she would be clearly seen in the window with her bundled "child" and would hopefully fool anyone watching the house that Mrs. Allinton was still at home.

She remained at the window but could not see beyond her reflection in the wavy glass. Out in the darkness, Mrs. Allinton would be racing to escape.

Lord God, she prayed, *please protect them.*

They weren't being followed, but Wilfrid Neybridge still kept vigilant watch of their surroundings as he drove the coach farther away from the Allinton's home and closer to the coaching inn where he had arranged to hire a post chaise. And not just one post chaise—he had arranged for two other carriages and two other drivers, and all three would leave the inn at the same time. If they managed to switch carriages quickly, anyone following would not know which one contained Mrs. Allinton and which were empty.

The wind was cold atop the box, and he huddled deeper into his heavy cloak. He hadn't posed as a coachman in some years, and had forgotten the chill and discomfort.

He laughed at himself. He was getting old indeed if he was complaining. It had always been the adventure that appealed to him, that made any discomfort into a mere trifle. He'd been afraid that returning to England would mire him in boring respectability, but first Dorothea and then Lena had ensured he was always entertained. The two girls, who were like daughters to him, kept him young. And serving as Lena's supervisor ensured he continued his clandestine work for England.

They reached the coaching inn, and Wilfrid drove the carriage as close to the stables as he could. He leaped down and opened the door, instructing Mrs. Allinton, "Hurry now. We must switch coaches as quick as can be."

Her face was white, but she nodded and obeyed quickly. She reminded Wilfrid of the soldiers he'd seen in France and Spain, fearful and yet brave enough to quickly respond to orders.

He and the two other post chaises left the coaching inn one after another, and each moved in a different direction at the crossroads.

It was another three hours of driving before they reached the outskirts of a small fishing village, a tiny place that would have been difficult to find if one were not looking for it, and even more difficult in the dark, but Wilfrid had always had an excellent sense of direction and keen eye for memorizing road marks. They descended a short rise to enter the village, and in the distance the sea was black, but the sky above it was a muted navy blue. Dawn would come in an hour or two.

He drove directly to the sea, parking the vehicle near the base of the natural wall of rocks that jutted out into the ocean and gave the small shoreline partial protection from the winds and waves.

From there, they walked along the deserted beach. Anyone watching them would have a difficult time spotting their figures out in the dark, but that also meant that they themselves had to be careful of their footing as they picked their way across the shoreline.

They finally reached a predetermined point and Wilfrid knelt, setting down the lantern he'd brought with him. It took him a few tries but he finally managed to light it with the flint he carried.

Standing and facing out to sea, he raised the lantern up and down three times.

Far off in the dark water, another light suddenly appeared and flickered on and off four times.

Wilfrid set the lantern on the ground and waited.

Mrs. Allinton had been quiet up until this point, but now she asked him in a low voice, "What is happening?"

"That's your water chariot, ma'am." Wilfrid adopted a casual country accent to hide his more genteel origins and nodded toward the bobbing light that was getting closer. "It'll take you to a fishing boat I've commissioned for you."

She was shaking her head. "Wherever it docks, they'll be there waiting for us."

"I doubt that. The fishing boat has directions to rendezvous with a merchant vessel that put out to sea a few hours ago."

Her mouth flew open. "Can they do that?"

"I've done it a time or two. Getting onto the merchant might be a tad rough, but they'll make sure you and the babe get on board safe and sound."

"But Stewart ..."

"He may already be waiting for you. He was to head straight for the coast and another fishing boat a few hours ahead of you."

"A merchant vessel ..." She stared out into the dark and

focused on the little light of the rowboat drawing closer to shore. "Where will it take us?"

"India, I believe. It was where Mr. Allinton wished to go."

"Will we be safe from *them* there?"

"I imagine so. And Mr. Allinton is quite clever."

She laughed then, a short breath. "Yes, he is." After another few minutes of listening to the wind, she asked, "That young woman who stayed behind for me … what will happen to her? Will she be safe?"

Wilfrid turned to her with a smile, although she likely couldn't see it in the gloom. "You needn't worry about my girl. She can handle herself."

A few hours earlier

Lena's peace was broken after only half an hour. She should have known the ever-hovering Burton wouldn't leave his mistress alone if she was in a distraught state, no matter if she told him she wished solitude or not.

A scratch at the door, then Burton entered with a small tea tray. "I know you wished to be alone, ma'am, but I thought a spot of tea might revive you. You mustn't stay awake too long, and I'm sure the babe …" He trailed off, and even though Lena's back was still to him, she could feel him staring holes into her.

"*You!*" He flung the accusation at her like a bullet.

She turned to him. His wide eyes blazed with wrath and also something that looked like panic. She would have expected a truly solicitous servant to wonder where his mistress had gone, but instead he was allowing his fury at her to leak out of him like a sieve.

She adopted a frightened, cowed posture, sidling away from the window and dropping the bundle of blankets she was carrying, holding it in front of her as if she were a child. "I was forced to do it."

He bared his teeth into a sneer. "I had suspected something when the woman leaving had known to avoid the creaking place on the stairs." Then his eyes widened. "And I didn't even notice you're wearing a dress and not her nightgown!" His hand clenched in frustration.

Lena continued to shy away from him, holding the blanket before her like a shield.

"Where did she go?"

"I don't know!" She injected high-pitched fright into her tone.

"I don't believe you!"

"It's the truth. They only paid me. They didn't tell me anything."

He lumbered toward her, his entire body tense with violence. "I'll *make* you tell me!" And he reached out to grab her throat.

Lena shot her forearm up and deflected his hand, then punched him solidly in the face.

Under the cover of the blanket, she'd donned several heavy silver rings that she always kept with her, so the blow broke his nose. She was glad of the hours of repetitive punching that her trainer, Mr. Armstrong, had always forced her to do with the wool and cloth-filled bag in the training room at the Ramparts, but hitting a man always hurt more than the bag, and her hand stung.

He reacted faster than she expected, but she easily ducked under his flying swing and moved slightly behind him. She grabbed at his arm, then pulled it back and used it like a lever to force him to the ground with a sudden, unexpected shove. The carpet wasn't thick enough to dull the pain as his head thudded onto the floor.

He gave a half-grunt, half-scream at her, but she set her foot against the back of his shoulder while still holding his arm twisted behind him. When he struggled, he immediately stopped as the angle at which she held him caused pain to shoot up his shoulder.

"I had been hoping you were simply an overly loyal servant or someone with a sweet spot for your mistress."

He called her a colorful name, but she'd heard it from other men before, most of them also held captive by her at the time.

"Who hired you to watch the family?" she demanded.

He told her rudely where to go, and she applied subtle pressure to his shoulder. He gave a short squeal, then hastily said, "I don't know."

"How could you not know?"

"They told me what to do by sending me messages through my sister. She has a house in Efford."

The neighboring village. "What did they tell you to do?"

"I had to send a note if the family looked like they were making plans to run away. And then the last time I did that, a man dropped off a bag of gold at my sister's house."

"Where did you send the note?"

He had started to calm down now, and tried to peer up at her from where his face was pressed against the floor. "Here now, that's information you need, isn't it? How about you give me a little something for my time, eh? What do you sa—eeeeeh, stop it! That hurts!"

"The address."

He gave it to her, accompanied by inarticulate grumbling noises.

For the past few minutes, she'd been aware of soft footsteps approaching from the bowels of the house, and now she looked up in time to see three women just reaching the open door. All three were still dressed, although only the oldest one still wore an apron over her dark skirts. The woman, probably the housekeeper, took in the situation with a gasp.

Then she did something Lena did not expect. She looked at her and asked, "Did he do something to you, miss?"

Lena had been expecting shock and confusion, perhaps a bit of hysteria, but certainly not that. She glared down at Burton, although he couldn't see her, and applied a little more pressure to his arm.

"Owowow stop that!"

"Are you the type of man to make a habit of intimidating women, you scum?"

"Whatever they say about me, I didn't do it!"

From the open doorway, the two maids and the housekeeper shot venomous glares at Burton.

Well, that answered her question.

With a friendly smile, Lena asked the housekeeper, "Might I bother you for a bit of rope?"

Burton immediately protested, "What are you going to do? I didn't do anything wron—owowow!"

"Much as I deplore it, you'll be released after I have done what I came to do," Lena told him.

The housekeeper, who introduced herself as Mrs. Fenwick, provided a nice length of strong rope, and with her help, Lena managed to get Burton tied to an ugly chair that Mrs. Fenwick said the mistress didn't particularly care for.

By this time, the one footman in the house had arrived. Burton appealed to him—apparently named Miles—with loud complaints, but the man simply frowned at him and ignored him.

"Now that the garbage is taken care of ..." Lena dusted off her hands. "Mrs. Fenwick, in the morning, please send a groom to Mr. Allinton's cousin, Mr. Lewis Allinton, and ask him to please come to the house as soon as possible."

"The elder Mr. Lewis Allinton? Mr. Allinton's next of kin?"

"Yes, precisely. I have been told his house is only an hour away, yes?"

Mrs. Fenwick nodded.

"I am afraid the Allintons will not be returning home. I have a letter from Mr. Allinton to his cousin, with a request for him to close up the house for him."

The maids were utterly confused at this turn of events, staring at Lena with round eyes. Mrs. Fenwick looked alarmed, but strove to remain calm.

"Mr. Allinton has not forgotten you." Lena reached into her pocket for the sheaf of papers she'd stashed there. "He has written references for all of you, and he has instructed Mr. Lewis Allinton to give all of you a month's wages. He also asks that you help his cousin with the house."

Mrs. Fenwick laid a relieved hand on her chest. "Mr. Allinton was always so thoughtful. Of course."

"What about me?" Burton seemed annoyed that Lena got along so well with Mrs. Fenwick.

She sifted through the papers, found his letter, and tore it into pieces. "You are being turned out without a reference, Mr. Burton. I do believe Mr. Allinton will not object to my high-handedness in this matter."

He glared at her and jerked at his ropes, but she had tied them expertly, and he was stuck to the chair.

"If you tip over, I shan't pick you back up again," Lena warned him.

Mrs. Fenwick said, "Miss ... er ..."

"Call me Mary, Mrs. Fenwick."

"Miss Mary, would you like a nice cup of tea? And I do believe we still have some lemon biscuits the cook made for Mrs. Allinton."

Lena glanced at the tea tray Burton had brought and didn't trust it. "I should love that, Mrs. Fenwick. Thank you."

"Miles, wake up the stable boy and have him help you carry this trash out of the house." Mrs. Fenwick gave Burton a frosty look. "The master's cousin will deal with him when he arrives."

Burton began protesting loudly, spitting out rude names for all of them and their ancestors.

"Where should I take him?" Miles asked.

She regarded Burton, who was still swearing up a storm.

"Take him out back behind the kitchens." She gave Burton a suddenly wicked smile. "I have a wonderful idea. Set him right next to the privy."

Chapter Nine

The church was one of the most ostentatious Lena had ever seen, and also the coldest. She shivered as she entered the empty sanctuary.

She was early for service, and she circled around the edge of the entire vast space, pretending to study the carvings on the walls for various well-heeled personages who were buried here. After she'd ascertained the entire space was indeed as empty as it looked, she headed toward a particular pew where she found a drunken man lying on the floor.

"You must be freezing." She sat in the pew.

"I've slept in worse places," Mr. Drydale groaned as he sat up, now that she had ascertained the sanctuary was indeed empty of prying eyes.

"No one?"

"Not a single person all night."

Lena avoided looking at a different pew, across the aisle and one seat further forward, where Mr. Drydale had deposited the item that Mr. Allinton's letter writer had been so desperate to trade for.

Directly after capturing Mr. Gordon, Mr. Drydale had accompanied Mr. Allinton to his fishing boat at a tiny village on the coast, then had ridden all night to London in order to place the item inside St. Julia's, a small but snobbish church in

Mayfair, as per the instructions Mr. Allinton had received. He had then posed as a drunk sleeping off a night of revelry, in the event a priest or parishioner discovered him, in order to keep a covert eye upon the package.

But no one had arrived all night. Before delivering the item, he had left a note for Lena to attend services if they had not heard from Mr. Drydale by then.

He sat next to Lena, smoothing down his wrinkled coat and settling his hat upon his head. It had not gotten crushed since he had placed it on the pew bench. "I'm assuming everything went well?"

He was referring to Mrs. Allinton. "Yes." She wasn't certain if she was allowed to ask him what the item had been until they were in more private surroundings, so she didn't mention it, but he answered her unspoken question anyway in a low voice.

"It was a jade box, exquisitely carved. Oriental make. This was inside." He handed her a small cloth pouch.

She nearly dropped it in an automatic reaction. Inside was what looked like little brown dried caterpillars, but on closer inspection they were not insects, but some type of herb. Or perhaps a mushroom, from the smell. It was like nothing she'd ever seen. "What is it?"

"I have an appointment with some experts later today."

"You ... left the box?"

"Couldn't reproduce it in so little time. Replaced the herb with something I found in an apothecary's shop that looked somewhat similar, if less aromatic." Mr. Drydale covered his mouth with his hand to hide his yawn, then doffed his hat to her and left the church.

She only had to wait another fifteen minutes or so before another parishioner arrived for services, and then a rush of people paraded in, dressed in fine but understated clothing appropriate for Sunday services. She watched the pew without appearing to watch it, and while an old woman and her younger grandson or grand-nephew sat on the near end, no one sat on the far end where the item had been tucked underneath.

She was surprised at how many people came to St. Julia's for worship on Sunday, although the majority of them seemed to enjoy gossiping with each other as opposed to preparing their hearts and minds for a divine message while waiting for the service to start. She sighed. She had been like that once, long, long ago.

The service began, but Lena kept her eye on the pew. And so she noticed when a gentleman arrived late for the service while everyone was standing and singing.

He was of average height but a bit slender, and his carriage was slightly stooped even though he was no older than Wilfrid. His sandy-brown hair was cut fashionably like most other gentlemen, and his shirt-points were only modestly high. He wore a brown jacket and buff waistcoat embroidered with gold, both extremely fine quality that fit him very well, making him fit in perfectly with the other wealthy people around him.

He slipped into the church and made an effort to muffle the sound of the door closing. As he walked down the outside aisle, he smiled genially to everyone he met, but like a stranger would to other strangers. He did not normally attend this church.

He sat on the pew directly on top of where the box had been stowed.

He apparently was accustomed to church services, for he was not awkward as he stood and sat and sang the hymn. His eyes were slightly glazed as they stared at the rector, but he did not look around with a bored expression or whisper with his neighbor, like others were doing. However, she saw the moment he stooped to retrieve the package, doing it in such a way that no one would have noticed, not even the old woman and young man on the same pew.

It was not difficult to follow him after the service ended. He stepped out onto the fashionable street and turned right, his coat swinging at an awkward angle from something large stuffed into a pocket.

It was when he turned right at the next corner that it became difficult, not because Lena lost sight of him, but because the street he turned onto was more congested. Despite being close to the wealthier section of London, just a single street over, the pedestrians were of a slightly more common stamp, arms held close against pickpockets.

She kept his head in view, able to spot his beaver hat easily in the crowd, but something about the many people around him made her uneasy, and she couldn't quite understand why. He never stopped or spoke to anyone, he never looked in shop windows or bought anything from the street vendors. He kept walking.

Then he turned right at another corner. And then turned left at the next. Now he was back on the street that ran in front of St. Julia's, but walking in the opposite direction. And she realized he had deliberately detoured from the church onto that street, walking in a not-quite-complete circle.

Something had happened. Something she'd *missed*.

He kept walking. His home was rather far from St. Julia's, but still at a very exclusive address in Grosvenor Square.

It was harder to follow him with fewer people on the streets, so she paused to remove her cloak, then flipped it around. The inner lining had deliberately been made of plainer, coarser wool. She ruthlessly plucked the feathers and flowers from her bonnet, leaving the plain dark blue ribbon around the crown. She continued to follow him, but now she looked more like an upper servant such as a lady's maid, a common enough sight on these streets and more easily overlooked.

She was able to follow him directly to his townhouse, only a few yards behind him. It was as he climbed the steps to his front door that she realized his coat now hung differently around him than it had when he'd left the church. Before, it had hung heavier on his right side, but now it was lighter.

She remembered the crowd of people around him on that street, and his deliberate detour. She remembered the uneasy feeling she had, and now knew she'd been right.

Except there was nothing she could have done. There had been too many people around him, too many people who passed next to him, to be able to know who had picked his pocket for the box.

She kept walking down the street as his butler let him in the front door, greeting him.

"Welcome home, Mr. Farrimond."

Chapter Ten

"'Nothing.'" Sir Derrick skewered Sol with those intent, slightly bulging eyes, the whites bright against his tanned skin, and repeated what Sol had said to him. His tone was incredulous and yet also somehow made him feel like an imbecile.

"Nothing, sir," Sol repeated.

"Absolutely nothing?"

"We had two teams of agents search his house."

Sir Derrick gave a long sigh and sat back in his chair in his office, glaring at the ceiling. "Miss Penrose is certain it was Mr. Farrimond?"

"Her description matches him, and she heard his butler greeting him when he arrived at a certain townhouse that is his address."

Sir Derrick gave another long sigh, and this time, Sol echoed it.

His disappointment burned hotter because they'd been so hopeful when Miss Penrose returned from following him. Mr. Farrimond was on the list of possible Foreign Office moles that Sol had been investigating.

However, she had spoken frankly about the man's strange walking detour and her impression that the box, which had been in his coat pocket, had been taken from him by the time he had entered his townhouse. Sol had had agents sneak in to search his house that very night, but they had not found the box, nor had they found anything to indicate he might be the mole, let alone Allinton's letter-writer.

If someone had picked Farrimond's pocket on his way home, they would have known immediately that the herb within was fake. Within the hour, that "someone" would have deduced that the seller must have been caught, so in that sense, they had been a few hours ahead of Sol and his team in terms of cleaning up his trail.

"We've had men watch the boarding house where the butler, Burton, had been sending his notes about the Allintons," Sir Derrick said. "No one has come to claim the false note we left."

"Whether Farrimond is a mole or not doesn't help us to discover who within the Ramparts knew Allinton's skill with safes," Sol said.

Sir Derrick gave a heavier sigh before sliding another folder across the desk at Sol. "Did you hear about Cridale?"

"His suicide? Yes, Nell just told me. I was shocked." He opened the folder and scanned the contents, then immediately grew still.

The symbol stared up at him.

"We found this in his house barely an hour ago. It's another note apparently for Allinton, with another safe to open for him."

"*Cridale* was the letter writer? He was the one who betrayed Allinton to Gordon?" Sol shook his head. "No, I can't believe it."

"I rarely believe anything," Sir Derrick said. "Excessive distrust of everything is the only means to success in this business. But apparently it's true."

Sol slid the folder back to him. "The man is conveniently dead, and things like this can be planted in his home."

"That's why I wanted to ask you about Gordon. Did he say anything about the client with whom he arranged the trade?"

"No. He said he never met them face to face."

"Is he telling the truth?"

"He seemed to be ..."

Sir Derrick noticed his hesitation. "But ...? Out with it, man."

"I suspect he recognized the symbol when I showed it to him."

Sir Derrick stared at the letter in Cridale's folder. "Allinton's notes were signed with this symbol, and so was that letter your man Ackett found in the desk of Napoleon's aide."

Something occurred to Sol. "Did you confirm the two were exactly the same?"

"It was not perhaps made with exactly the same stamp, but it is the same symbol." Sir Derrick frowned. "Gordon didn't know anything about who—or *whom*—are behind that stamp?"

"He might know, but he was afraid of them. He fully admitted it."

"He wouldn't say why? Do they have something they're holding over him, like with Allinton?"

Sol shook his head. He didn't know.

"Where is he now?" Sir Derrick asked.

"We arranged for a certain cell in Newgate and put him in under a false name."

"You decided to hide him like a needle in a haystack?" Sir Derrick made a contemplative frown. "Clever. Might even work."

"I'll visit him in another day or two, after he's had a taste of Newgate. By then, he might be more amenable to things like food and a nice fire."

Sir Derrick closed the folder. "If Mr. Ackett hadn't found that note to Napoleon, this wouldn't be so complicated."

"We wouldn't be thinking about treason, for one."

"What does Farrimond have to do with Cridale? I didn't think they even knew each other."

Sol had no answer for him.

Sir Derrick now stared at a different closed file on his desk. "That herb we took from the box ..."

"I have an appointment to meet with Lowald and Brady later today about it."

"You don't think … That couldn't possibly have to do with the strength elixir that group was offering to Napoleon?"

"I think it unlikely."

Sir Derrick's eyebrows rose. "Oh?"

"When they offered it to Napoleon in that letter, they would have already had it. They even offered a demonstration at his earliest convenience. Yet they went through great pains to force Allinton to steal rare and unusual objects in order to trade for that herb. They would need to find some other means of acquiring more, which would be presumably just as difficult, in order to make more of the elixir, if that herb is a key ingredient. If this group's leaders are smart, they wouldn't leave that key ingredient to chance like that."

Sir Derrick was nodding thoughtfully. "We don't know if they're smart. I know you think they might be a threat, but their claims are far-fetched. I'm more interested in the mole in the Foreign Office who delivered the note for them, if it's Farrimond or not."

"Yes, sir."

"Super-strength elixir." Sir Derrick gave a scornful snort. "Preposterous."

Newgate stank.

Maxham was particularly sensitive to smell, so the odor burned his nose like breathing in an oven. Breathing through his mouth only made him taste the stench, which was even worse.

Unfortunately, the cell that he sought was quite far from the entrance. A very many coins in a guard's palm led him to the bars in front of a large, dark room filled with despair. The scent of hopelessness was even stronger than the foul odors.

He wore his usual nondescript gray and brown, but he shone

like a beacon in that dank place, and the man he sought spotted him immediately, but didn't recognize him since they had never met.

"Gordon," Maxham said.

The man shot to his feet. Even in the darkness, Maxham could see a warring of fear and hope in his eyes. Shoving aside the other prisoners who came up to the bars to reach for Maxham, Gordon pleaded with him, "Please, I didn't tell them anything."

Maxham smiled gently and stroked the back of Gordon's hand where it gripped the black iron bars. "I know you didn't." The man had known precisely to whom he was selling that box and its precious contents. Even others far less wise wouldn't speak of Maxham's group, because they simply knew things and used that knowledge to their advantage in creative ways.

The man suddenly stared at the hand he was stroking. Maxham couldn't feel it through his leather gloves, but the paste that Jack had smeared on the palm would have become absorbed into his skin by now.

Panic flared in his eyes, bright like the spark from a hot, quick-burning fire, quick to die out. "No! Please! I didn't tell them anything!" He began scrubbing his hand on his dirty trousers.

"I'm afraid we couldn't do anything too obvious." Maxham stripped off the glove and tossed it into a corner where a puddle of black water pooled. He took another glove from his pocket and tugged it on. "Jack tells me it's not a poison, but it will make you very nauseous. You won't be able to swallow anything, including water. And in here ..." Maxham cast his eyes over the fetid surroundings. "You won't last more than a day or two."

"No! Please!"

Maxham turned and walked away from the dying man's screams.

Chapter Eleven

"Are you certain?" Maxham asked in his faltering Chinese.

"Of course I am certain!" the Chinese man retorted. "Do you think I am dim-witted?"

"Keep your voice quiet." They were meeting in the woods outside the laboratory so that Ward wouldn't know that Maxham was talking to his assistant, Lee. Even if they were overheard, Ward wouldn't know what they were talking about because he had never bothered to learn Chinese, even though he'd brought Mr. Lee all the way from China in order to help him with his experiments. He treated Lee like a slave rather than an assistant, so it had been pitifully easy for Maxham to gain the man's trust.

But Ward would suspect *why* Maxham wanted to speak to his assistant, and would assume he was after the formulation. Which wouldn't be far off the mark, and Maxham didn't want to have to deal with Ward's suspicions and anger. All that sort of stuff was very untidy.

Lee upended the jade box and shook the herb out onto the ground, his movements jerky and angry. "This is not 冬虫夏草菌. It is nothing but common weed."

Maxham was not yet proficient in Chinese, so he didn't know the translation of the word Lee had used. "What is it, exactly?" Lee had originally mentioned it was a form of mushroom.

"In your tongue it would be …" He paused, then said in halting English, "Caterpillar fungus."

Maxham couldn't prevent a grimace of disgust.

Lee immediately took offense. "It is highly prized! It is used to replenish the kidneys and soothe the lungs, which I desperately need after so long in this cold, wet country." He wrapped his cloak more tightly about his slim frame. "It is expensive and difficult to find even in China. The man you bought it from must have been trying to trick you."

It had been extremely difficult to find anyone who even knew what he'd been looking for, and Gordon, the one person he'd found, had had some ridiculous demands before he would trade.

Maxham hadn't liked dealing with Gordon, who usually only dealt in gemstones, but the man had happened to acquire the box and herb as an oddity among other more valued items in a business deal, and Maxham had run out of sources for the rare Chinese medicinal ingredient.

However, all things considered, Maxham had been rather fortunate that he'd realized the herb might have been switched out almost immediately. He'd checked the contents right away after taking the box from Farrimond's pocket, as they'd arranged, and he'd seen the green-colored vegetation within. He knew the mushroom that Lee desired was light brown with a darker stem, and this was obviously not it.

He considered the possibility that Gordon had been mistaken, but when they were corresponding, the man had sent a rather well-drawn picture of the herb so that Maxham would know he was receiving what he had asked for, and this looked nothing like the drawing.

"I think Gordon did have the true herb, but when I saw that it was different, the only conclusion I could draw was that the box had been intercepted and the contents replaced, and that Gordon was likely captured."

Lee frowned. "Captured for selling fungus?"

"What he wanted in exchange wasn't money."

Lee cast a nervous glance through the woods in the direction of the laboratory building. "Did he know who he was trading with?"

"He did." Maxham had done business with Gordon many times before. "But I took care of it."

Lee relaxed. He may not like Ward, but he also enjoyed the experiments they were doing—they were a challenge to him, and his lifestyle here was significantly better than his circumstances had been in China. He didn't wish any of that to end, which would happen if Maxham's group was discovered.

Still, he had gotten his hopes up about the Caterpillar Fungus. He scowled at the box and handed it back to Maxham.

The box was exquisite, hand-carved from palest green jade in two pieces, the box and the cover. The hinges were only made of brass, however, and had started to turn green.

Lee began stomping back to the laboratory. "This is your fault. I had been looking forward to the 冬虫夏草菌."

Maxham sucked on his bottom lip as he regarded the jade container. "Well ... at least it's a pretty box."

"It's some type of fungus," Mr. Lowald said.

"Probably grown in the Far East since it was in the jade box," Mr. Brady added.

Sol barely managed to restrain himself from saying, *Brilliant deduction.* It was difficult enough dealing with Lowald and Brady, who were both eccentric, haughty, and easily offended.

But they were two scientists often used by the Ramparts for their knowledge and discretion. Sol found them unpleasant, and didn't quite trust them, but they were the only men whose background and loyalties had been approved by the Ramparts who could help him.

"What is it used for?" Sol asked, trying not to grit his teeth in frustration.

"Don't know," Lowald said. Brady also shook his head.

"You said it was a fungus? Like a mushroom?"

"Not quite, but close," Lowald said with a superior sniff.

"So perhaps it was used as a poison?" Sol said.

"It could have been used as a medicine ..." Brady suggested, but Lowald shot him down.

"Who'd use a mushroom for medicine? Don't be daft. It was most likely used as a poison."

"Could you find out?" Sol asked.

"How?" Lowald snorted. "Do you know how many poisons there are? And some medicines are poison in certain doses. We don't know the first thing about what we're dealing with here."

"And you know those Oriental people," Brady added. "They eat strange things."

"I'm certain most of those Oriental medicines are poisons," Lowald said.

Then before Sol could stop him, Lowald tossed the entire sack of herb into the fireplace. Fortunately, it didn't explode or flare.

"What are you doing?" Sol demanded. "If it is a poison, as you say, you've just sent it into the air. You could have killed us all."

"All poisons are easily burned and rendered inactive," Lowald said loftily, but Sol was fairly certain he was wrong about that.

He stared at the burning sack of Chinese fungus and sighed.

Connect with Camy

I hope you enjoyed *The Gentleman Thief*! Originally, I had thought I should have this prequel story as part of the first book in my series, *Lady Wynwood's Spies, volume 1: Archer*. However, the other books in the series are very long, about 100,000 words each, while this story was very short, and I didn't want to add subplots just to beef up the word count.

I decided to write this as a prequel novella, even though I had already had *The Spinster's Christmas* as a full-length prequel novel. So now I have two prequel books, which I know is kind of strange but at this point in my life, I'm not afraid of being strange! LOL

I hope you enjoy the rest of the Lady Wynwood's Spies series! Sign up for my email newsletter (https://bit.ly/lady-wynwood) to be sure to hear when the next book in the series is available.

Camy

Made in the USA
Columbia, SC
27 March 2024

33688497R00076